MY PAPER HALF

MY PAPER HALF

Shirshendu Mukhopadhyay

Translated from the Bengali novel *Kagojer Bou* by

Soma Das

NIYOGI BOOKS

Published by
NIYOGI BOOKS
D-78, Okhla Industrial Area, Phase-I
New Delhi-110 020, INDIA
Tel: 91-11-26816301, 49327000
Fax: 91-11-26810483, 26813830
email: niyogibooks@gmail.com
website: www.niyogibooksindia.com

Editor: Mohua Mitra
Cover Design: Arrt Creations
Layout: Shashi Bhushan Prasad

ISBN: 978-93-83098-52-1
Publication: 2014

Printed at: Niyogi Offset Pvt. Ltd., New Delhi, India

One

How did the word 'glutton' come about? What is the history behind the word 'snitch'? Come to think of it, why is 'shameless' such a derogatory word? Of course, dishonour would be of consequence only if one made room for it. In my situation, to take humiliation to heart would be a luxury in itself.

I slept in the rear veranda of Subinoy's house. Surrounded by a chest-high wall topped with grills to the ceiling, it was not too bad a place. Half the veranda was shielded with planks of plywood into a dining room of sorts. In the other half was a washbasin; the used utensils from dinner and some empty packing boxes kept it company. Chemicals were imported in these boxes and, being of foreign make, they were quite sturdy. During the day these boxes – three in all – were stacked to a side. At night I laid them side by side to make myself a bed of sorts. Since the boxes were not of the same height the bed was quite uneven. But half a loaf was better than none—I found this arrangement better than sleeping on the floor. I quite liked the slight elevation.

There were two rooms adjoining the veranda. In one room Subinoy's widowed mother lived; she slept in a bed while the teenaged maid, Kusum, slept on the floor. In the other room there were two beds. Subinoy slept in one while his wife, Khawna, shared the other with their two children. Towards the front of the house were a couple more rooms—one was Subinoy's laboratory while the other was a living room. But it never crossed anyone's mind to offer me the use of any of those rooms. Subinoy had a sister who had, till recently, been deprived of marital bliss. And the longer the wait to tie the knot stretched, the more she immersed herself in caring for her appearance. The sight of any young male always sent her into frenzy and, eventually, when she came to focus her attention on a good-for-nothing like me, the alarm bells went off in my head! One day, she very clearly asked her sister-in-law, "Even in this cold weather Upal-da sleeps in the open veranda. Why don't you let him sleep in the dining room?" During the course of this conversation I was seated a couple of feet away, at the dining table, having tea with Subinoy. I stole a glance and found Subinoy's sister, Achala, standing at the door to the kitchen. Khawna, seated on a stool within, gave her a meaningful look and said, "Um … hmm!"

And immediately, the import dawned on me. Of course! The shelves in the dining room were stacked with steel utensils; there were so many little items, like spoons, which could easily be pilfered. It would have been foolish on their part to let me sleep there.

Anyway, to come back to Achala, one night, when she was in the grip of that frenzy, she almost made arrangements to oust me from this shelter of mine. Without rhyme or reason, she appeared in the veranda. I slept by the passage leading to the toilet and she could have very well passed me by on her way there. But no, she did not intend to use the toilet. She homed in on me, and standing very close to my packing-box bed heaved a heavy sigh. Well, the sigh could have been an expression of nothing but humane pity but it broke my light sleep and, taking her to be a ghost, I screamed, "Oh my god!"Achala managed a timely escape but made a fair deal of noise while shutting her bedroom door. Subinoy's mother woke up due to the commotion and came to the veranda to investigate. Though I explained that

I was frightened by a nightmare she did not buy the story. She declared in the air, perhaps for my ears, "This is not good. I shall have to tell Subinoy tomorrow."

I have no clue what she said to her son but Subinoy simply brushed the matter aside. Else, I would have been in a soup; Subinoy was built like a giant and when angered he lost his grip on himself. He was a man who dwelled in his own world, a world of thought, not caring much for the problems seeking his attention. Worldly affairs irritated him. The fact that I was staying in his house and feeding off him was not looked upon with favour by his family; but such things were beyond Subinoy's comprehension. He was immersed in chemistry, all the time. He was the chief chemist in a renowned company and had also gathered enough fame by authoring commendable papers. He travelled abroad often and belonged to the rare breed of Bengali husbands whose wives held them in reverence. In my lifetime, I was yet to see another case where the wife respected her husband. And it was because of the authority Subinoy wielded that I had managed to enjoy this shelter so far. Well, there was also a secret reason behind Subinoy not asking me to leave.

But it would be wrong for anyone to conclude that Subinoy had a soft corner for me. It was true that we had spent our schooldays together in Mitra Institution; at the time, we were very close friends. In college, he took up science while I opted for commerce. I somehow managed to scrape through my BCom course and then drew the line as far as academics were concerned. But Subinoy graduated with a gold medal and charged forth. We went our separate ways. When one of two friends revelled in success, companionship usually gave way to complications.

Now, all and sundry knew me as quite a worthless man. Unfortunately, it took a long while for that fact to dawn on me. I always believed that someday my talent would come to light. I was a fair enough singer, a good enough painter and a brilliant actor; I had also written a few plays on the pitiful plight of refugees; but what I was best at was creating clay sculptures. This multitude of talents had always preserved my faith in myself that I would taste success along one avenue or another. And if I could triumph in all those fields then that would be the icing on the cake. But others held to their own beliefs. My adroit father said, "This boy will not achieve anything. How can one succeed when his attention is divided among so many things?"

My family history is quite brief. I was the only child of my parents. When I was five my mother passed away, upon which my father married my Mashi or aunt—my mother's cousin sister who had been written off the matrimonial roster because she was blind in one eye and sported protruding front teeth. Mashi brought me up. Before my BCom final examinations my father passed away; and then, in the whole wide world, Mashi and I were left with none but each other to call our own. But neither of us could provide for the other. Mashi often lamented, "If only you could beg, borrow or steal and bring in a few paise!"

I had heard that man matured and progressed in various ways with age. But I seemed to be an exception. Yes, I could still sing like before, given an opportunity would act well and could pen a play or two even today. I could very well paint a picture or craft a figurine from clay. Yet, those talents too seemed to have stagnated; they had lost out on enhancement. At a time, I tried acting in films. I managed to land a couple of negligible roles but that could not be signified as film-acting. I also landed two jobs—one was lost as the company went out of business while the other was only temporary and died a predestined death. In her time, Mashi had been sparingly educated. After the demise of my father she toiled over tailoring work to make ends meet; and, in the process, almost spoilt her good eye. But when Mashi cried, even her blind eye welled over.

Through the day I used to wander, having no work. Actually, I enjoyed it. The lack of work ushered in languor and there was no dearth of companions to while away the hours nattering. Dumping the worries of domesticity on Mashi, I spent my days outside. And when there was no one to keep me company, I watched magic shows in the Maidan, enjoyed the free-for-all football and cricket matches around the city and leafed through magazines at the USIS library. My father had not provided us with a roof over our heads. And the time came when, following up on overdue rent, the landlord threw us out. The old landlord had died and his sons did not have many sympathetic bones in their bodies. To escape the miserable plight, Mashi requested refuge with a wealthy cousin brother. He did not disappoint Mashi. After all, poor cousins could always be put to some use. But I was not as lucky.

The family said, "We cannot put up your nephew. He is an adult and can fend for himself."

Mashi said, "What do you mean by nephew? He is my son! I have brought him up."

But they were adamant. Mashi sobbed copiously and after comforting her with a volley of false consolations I made my escape. Whatever fate might have in store for me, at least my blind Mashi would not starve to death. But I did visit her in that house and even enjoyed a few meals upon invitation.

At the time, I was a ticket conductor on the Howrah-Kadamtala bus route. Amidst the daylong jingle of coins, the swarm of sweaty bodies and the snarling traffic I never felt that I was a graduate and a simple clerk's job would have been more favourable. Anyway, the job was not too bad though I did not come out with flying colours from the arguments with passengers. There was a plus side to the job—I managed to keep myself updated on world affairs free of cost while listening in on the conversations of the passengers. Within a few days, I gathered who lorded over which area. Let alone asking them to buy tickets, I actually indulged them more often than not. Manai Ghosh was such a one. Once, the bus had to wait for him at Panchanantala while he fetched his clothes from the laundry. I also made the acquaintance of the area's petty thieves and pickpockets. To this day, whenever I visit, I am certain of a free cup of tea. As a novice I had coins stolen from my bag a couple of times. But, gradually, I adopted the cunning of a crow.

Dhan Singh was the driver of the bus. Once, he ran over a young boy near the water tank and a crowd started to chase the bus. Fear made Dhan Singh take leave of his senses; he raced the bus through the narrow and crowded streets, not stopping at any of the bus stops along the way. The passengers screamed and cursed in fear for their lives, "Help! You fool! You son of a swine!" But it all fell on deaf ears. Gobinda and me – the two conductors – stood glued to the doors, ready to take a leap at the first sign of danger. Dhan Singh almost flew the bus to Kadamtala but no sooner did he apply the brakes than people gathered in hundreds. There seemed to be no escape! Dhan Singh ended up in the hospital after being subjected to extreme assault while Gobinda and I lay on the roadside in a stupor after the blows stopped raining. Our faces swelled up and the aches all over felt like the burn of a hundred infected boils.

Much later, a few young boys who worked in a familiar roadside eatery provided us a drink of water and helped us up. The pair of us dragged ourselves to the eatery, moaning and groaning all the way. Our bags had vanished, our clothes were in tatters and Gobinda had even lost his slippers. There was nothing one could do in the face of public wrath. One couldn't even be angry—the mind could not summon up a face to fuel the anger. Yet the eyes filled up with tears of resentment against one's own life as well as the entire world. Gobinda and I ordered a quarter pound of bread and a half portion of mutton curry each. But the instant Gobinda put some curry into his mouth he yelped in agony and said, "I have a cut in my tongue … the spices are sending a jolt through it … how am I supposed to eat?"

Amidst such lamentation, one of the boys appeared and said, "Gobinda-da, a man from your village has been asking for you. Look, there he is again."

Gobinda looked up and I followed his gaze. An elderly man, weighed down by a morose expression on his facc, sat on the bench wiping the sweat on his face with a piece of white rag.

Gobinda asked, "Tarak-jetha, how are you? Any bad news?"

"Yes, son. Your father …"

Gobinda jumped up and interrupted, "Don't say anymore."

The man ground to a startled halt. I looked back to find Gobinda gobbling up the bread and mutton curry, the pain in his tongue forgotten. Through the mouthfuls, he said, "The news will spoil the meal. Right now I could polish off a horse. Please wait a while … that piece of news can be shared five minutes later. After all I am a Hindu by birth. How could I finish my meal after hearing those words?"

After finishing the meal, Gobinda paid for it and then said, "Let's go. I'll have to go to the village, won't I?"

Tarak-jetha sighed heavily and said, "Of course. It was the day before yesterday … your father returned from the fields and then, all of a sudden, lay down in the courtyard. Water, fan, the quack … oh dear….”

Gobinda brought his mouth close to my ear and said, “Upal, this is good news.”

Then he assumed a serious look and said, “It was time for him to leave. What did he stand to gain anymore? Life had already run dry for him.”

Saying this, he looked at me and said, “Upal, why don’t you come along? You’ll get to shed the body ache. Back in the village we are landed farmers. My father drove me out because of my wretched behaviour; there was no way I could go back. Else, why would I waste away as a ticket conductor?”

Giving up our jobs without notice, we headed for Shibganj in the district of Howrah.

It was in my nature to extract a mile when offered an inch. Gobinda’s native place was quite nice, a few hours’ bus ride from Bagnan. Upon getting there, I felt as if I had been looking for such a place all along. Though Gobinda’s family did not own vast stretches of crop fields, they had enough to make for two square meals a day. They also owned a coconut grove and the not-so-large family lived fairly well in their double-storied mud house.

Free of the headache of having to arrange for my meals, I let down my anchor. A seed of hope took root—perhaps I could spend the rest of my life here. Gobinda often said, “Let me see if I can get you settled here.” But within three months, Gobinda tied the knot and another couple of months later his face started to sport a sulk. He stopped speaking to me with the old camaraderie. I gathered that his wife had filled his ears; but I let the matter wash over me and spent another month there. Six months went by. One night, as we were returning from a stage show, Gobinda’s elder brother shone the torch to light the way and said to me in a tempered voice, "Yours is not the age to feed off others. Also, where will you find work in these rural areas? I suggest you try the Kolkata market again."

•

GOBINDA'S ELDER BROTHER, Nandadulal, wanted me to marry his daughter, Kamalini. But Kamalini was only twelve and no beauty either. Moreover, to me marriage seemed an unnecessary worry; so I did not agree. Had they asked me to stay on with them post marriage, I would perhaps have given it a thought. On the contrary, Kamalini's mother often goaded me into the odd errand and tried to hustle me into finding a job. Many times, I was sent to the market at Belpukur to sell their shrivelled coconuts. Once I was told to scorch an entire field to ready it for a crop of sugarcane. I disliked such hard work. And a wife would only add to the worries.

One monsoon night Gobinda's granary was raided by thieves. A large quantity of rice was stolen. In the morning, after a round of brouhaha, the entire family put their heads together and decided that from then on I would have to stand guard at night. How could a useless soul like me feed off them without contributing in any way?

I stood guard for a fortnight. And then, one night, the thieves returned. There were four or five dark men of whom a couple even appeared familiar. I was sitting in the veranda with a lantern and a stick and from time to time, I tapped the stick on the ground. Two stray dogs were dozing before me when the incident unfolded. The very sight of the thieves made me part ways with my wit. As the men surrounded me, I forgot how to use the stick. One of them said, "You rascal, we'll kill you and bury you in the field, remember that." The dogs barked weakly at first and then, wagging their tails, got busy welcoming the thieves. I followed suit and said with a grin, "What do you think, huh? Do I really stand guard? They forced me into it. Now you wrap up your job quickly while I keep an eye out for you."

While the thieves were busy at work, I grabbed an opportune moment and took to my heels with the lantern and the stick. Else, the following morning would have brought me too many hassles.

At the time, the stick and the lantern were my sole possessions. On hindsight I regretted not joining hands with the thieves and helping myself to some cash or utensils from Gobinda's house.

My father spent the major part of his life in a postman's job and then was promoted to a sorter of mails. Had he managed to rise to the next level, he could have been referred to as a gentleman; but, alas, he was not able to achieve that distinction. His passion was to eat well and to do so he borrowed from far and wide. Even his provident fund savings were depleted to half the amount in catering to this indulgence. Through my life, I saw him locked in an endless search for money. When all doors to money closed, he looked about the house like a policeman. He turned out the bedding, combed the wardrobe from top to bottom, rummaged through the kitchen and leafed through old letters looking for some forgotten money. And, on the odd occasion when he did find a five or ten paise coin, he exclaimed, "Here it is! Didn't I say so?" Mashi was quite irked by the domestic arrangements being sent for a toss by his combing operation. But Baba cared two pence; instead he often pulled Mashi's leg by singing, "Buzz away blind bee ...." My half-blind Mashi had come to be known as the 'blind bee'.

I inherited the trait from my father. I, too, liked to look for money anywhere and everywhere, at any hour of the day—at the marketplace, along the roadside, within the house. And often I have actually found a quarter or two. Not that I minded an unsuccessful search. The search itself gave me great pleasure, the kind of bliss people felt when they flew kites or sat waiting for fish to bite the bait.

Once, the day before a general strike – a *bandh* – my father was out shopping. At the time, our old landlord was alive. Seeing my father in the market, he exclaimed in surprise, "What is this? Didn't I see you shopping this morning? Why are you here again?" My father scratched his head and replied, "Since tomorrow the shops will be closed I thought I'd shop for tomorrow." The old man retorted, "Since the day is a *bandh*, it should be spent likewise. Can't you eat frugally just one day? Why do you need to waste money shopping twice in a day? Huh! If you can't save a paisa or two now then when will you do so? … After you have sired a litter? God knows when you will realise the importance of those two paise. You will have to repent in old age."

Since then, my father often joked, "If you can't save even two paise …!"

Though a joke, the lack of those two paise rendered Mashi homeless and she had to take refuge with her cousin, working as a maid. And I was left with nothing but a lantern and a stick to hold on to.

To be honest, the day I fled Gobinda's house, with the lantern and the stick as my sole possessions, my heart was very heavy. Actually, while in that house, I made some money. Often I sold the odd household item and once even chanced upon a gold earring on the floor. I also helped myself to a few coins lying unclaimed. That secret treasure of mine was stashed away in the rafters of the western room of Gobinda's house. But alas, I could not bring it with me.

Two

Last night, Subinoy and Khawna were up late, talking about me. Khawna wanted to be rid of me, she did not wish to see me in this house another day. After a while, she said to her husband, "This morning, after you returned from the market, you put thirty-five paise on the table. I saw it with my own eyes. In fifteen minutes, the money had vanished. That shameless glutton of a friend of yours is quite a snitch!"

Subinoy said in a sleepy voice, "Why don't you put money away safely?"

"Oh dear, what a solution! How much safety can one adopt if a thieving glutton roams the rooms through the day? I say, you ask him to leave … it has been long enough. Today it was you who went to the market but usually that bosom friend of yours does the daily shopping. Who knows how much he pockets from the expenses."

As they talked, I left my packing-box bed and put my ear to the door to catch every word. The words were offensive but I couldn't fathom exactly to what extent. Moreover, they were not meant for my ears hence there was perhaps no reason for me to feel slighted.

Later, as I lay on my bed and gazed at the sliver of the moon through the grill, sleep took leave. How could I explain to them that, once in a while, I too needed a few paise? Of late, my greatest problem was that my mind was always fearful of hunger. Through the day, a hunger pang lay dormant in my belly. Even when I ate my fill, traces of that hunger still lingered. I was always worried—would I get food the next time I felt hungry?

My other problem was money. My life seemed to be dedicated to the sole task of searching for money. And I have been doing just that since I left Gobinda's house that night with the lantern and the stick. But money, too, appeared to have found countless ways to hoodwink me and carry on with its game of hide and seek.

A couple of days after fleeing with lantern and stick, I made the acquaintance of three petty thieves at the bus station in Bagnan. As we got talking I gathered a lot of information. They were doing pretty well from thieving, mugging and small-time robberies. After much pleading and nagging I managed to latch on to them. They, of course, warned me that if I dared to inconvenience them, I would have to bid my life farewell.

One afternoon, as we sat in the marketplace in Bagnan, I noticed a little girl heading for the shops with a young maid. One of the thieves, Kadam said, "That little girl is the homeopathy doctor Kalipada Ghosh's younger daughter. She is wearing a pair of gold earrings. Would you like to try, Upal?" The proposal made my limbs go numb. To be honest, there was a certain fool who was always ready to put a wedge into everything I attempted; that fool was my conscience. It often appeared unbidden and yapped away about morality and similar virtues. I could neither chase it away nor avoid it.

Another of the three, Haju, pinched me hard and said, "We have been feeding you for the past two days ... shouldn't you do something in return? Go on, get to work. If you are caught and thrashed then that, too, will be a valuable lesson, a part of this profession. Often enough you will have to take a beating. No use acting like a gentleman."

Of course ... they were right. The uncontrollable hunger pangs filled me with fear. Why should anyone feed me if I did not work? Thinking along those lines, I got up.

Since I knew the little girl to be Kalipada Ghosh's daughter, it made the approach easier. The girl bought some cooking fat which she collected in a battered aluminium bowl; as soon as she stepped onto the road I barred her way.

"Hey little girl, what's up with Kalipada-da? I have been asking him to give me a medicine for bellyache for a long time now…."

Surprised, the girl replied, "Baba is in Kharagpur."

Happy with the answer, I asked, "Can you place me? I am Ram-kaka, I live in Raghu's house by the level crossing. Do you know him?"

She nodded hesitantly. She knew.

I said, "Your father had asked me for a few things but I never got around to giving them to him. I have stored them in Mohin's shop. Why don't you come along and get them?"

Saying this, I proceeded to lead her through the market. The young maid, wiser in the ways of the world, suddenly spoke up, "Hey Binti, don't go. This man is not good."

I flared up, "I'll slap you … you wretched hussy! Just the other day Kalipada-da was telling me about the young maid in his house who's a thief. He must have been talking about you!"

Fear silenced the maid. My wits had always been sharp and ideas played around quite nicely in my head. Fear and faith, combined, made the little girl go along with me; soon the maid followed us into the narrow lane behind the shops. Having bought a fruit mixture from the grocer, I handed the small paper bag to the girl and said, "Give this to your father and mention my name. He will know."

The girl nodded. With the paper bag in hand she stared at me curiously. As she turned to go, I called her back and said, "Binti, don't your parents have any sense? They have allowed their little girl to step out wearing gold earrings? Come here … take them off and put them in the paper bag. Who knows when some ruffian will come along and snatch them away? Just yesterday someone got mugged here."

The little girl stood woodenly. The maid rasped, "Why should she take them off? You are trying to be clever, aren't you?"

I scolded her again. But Binti did not have a mind to take the earrings off. She shook her head and said, "No, I won't take them off. I have had my ears pierced recently. If I take out the earrings the holes will fill up."

Her words had reason. And in that scenario, how could I have taken her earrings?

The third one of the thieves was Pailen. He was a man of action with few words to spare. I gave the girl and her maid my consent to leave and they were on their way, when Pailen appeared and blocked the lane. He was dressed in a lungi and a vest; though thin, he was of strong build. He steered clear of manipulations. Instead, shoving the maid to the ground, he said, "If you scream I shall stamp on your neck and cut your breath off."

The scene made Binti tremble and she seemed to have lost her voice. Pailen swiftly removed her earrings and said, "Go home. If you open your mouth about this, I'll kill you."

As we walked towards the railway station, Pailen said to me, "You dunce, do tricks work all the time? If you can get the job done by flexing your muscles, why beat about the bush?"

Quite true.

They did not give me a share of the money that came in from the sale of the earrings. After all, my foolishness had very nearly botched the job.

One day, the four of us boarded the Panshkura-Howrah local train hoping for an opportune moment. It was Saturday evening and the carriages were rather sparsely filled. In one carriage there was an elderly couple. The lady was covered in jewellery. In recent times I had not seen anyone so heavily laden—bangles, a thick necklace, large earrings and prominent rings on the fingers. An invitation to thieves and muggers.

In the almost empty carriage, the old man appeared restless. We took seats opposite them and pretending to be asleep, watched them through half-closed eyes. The man said in an undertone, "It was a bad idea for you to leave home with so much jewellery on you. I am feeling uneasy."

The lady scoffed, "Stuff your fear! Have I ever stepped out without my jewellery? That is not in my nature."

Then she took out a sparkling steel container used to store betel leaves and condiments. It was a wonderful article with twelve compartments filled with as many types of condiments, and in the centre were the betel leaves wrapped in a moist cloth. A very expensive item.

Pailen and Haju readied themselves while Kadam and I stationed ourselves at each end of the carriage. Pailen had a pistol on him and Haju carried a dagger. Kadam was armed with a revolver but for some reason they did not deem it necessary to adorn me with a weapon. Early on, Haju had taught me how to hold two sharp blades in the gaps between my fingers and had said, "Watch the fun when you swipe your hand over someone's cheek with the blades in position. Blood gushing forth like a stream."

As soon as Pailen flashed the pistol, the old man exclaimed, "There you go! Didn't I say so? Now we are done for!"

The lady stuffed a betel leaf into her mouth and said, "Is this wretch a robber? Oh dear … but a while ago he was dozing away!"

The man replied in a low voice, "The dozing is over. Now you guard the fort!"

The lady rasped, "Why should I, when I have got a man with me? There was a time when you wielded the stick quite well. Don't you turn tail now!"

Pailen lost his patience and interrupted, "There isn't time for so many words, be quick. We are in a hurry."

The lady snarled, "That is quite evident. But I am not taking my jewellery off. If you are in a hurry then you may leave."

Haju barked at her to shut up and then, touching the point of his dagger to the old man's neck, he said, "I'll give you five minutes to take them off. If you dally, this old man will be done in, granny. You'll become a widow."

Granny choked on her betel leaf and, after a couple of hiccups, screamed dramatically, "Oh dear! Everyone come and see what is happening here. They are going to kill this old man!"

Less than twenty people were scattered within the carriage. None moved a muscle. Each sat still as a statue, either in preoccupation or in fear. Except for two young chaps who sneered from a corner, "How much is your commission? Hey brother, how much does the authority take away? Everything works to a plan, doesn't it?"

Grandpa, held at dagger-point, blustered, "What's wrong with you? Aren't you bothered? How many minutes of the five are left? Take off everything quickly!"

Granny was still reeling from the bout of choking. She hiccupped thrice and then said tearfully, "Why should I? Tell me who is going to replace this jewellery. Will you?"

"Yes, I will … I will. Now take them off, quick," grandpa hurried her.

Yet, granny remained nonchalant. She struggled to drag a few bangles from her wrist to her knuckles and then said, "It's been ages since I put them on. Now I have gained weight … it's not easy to slide them off!"

Haju handed his dagger to Pailen and took the pistol from him. Pailen slid the dagger under the bangle and cut it off swiftly. Granny started to scream in fear but Pailen was a seasoned player—he hadn't dealt a single scratch. He quickly proceeded to cut off one bangle after another.

Granny looked at grandpa and said through her tears, "You have promised! You will have to get me exactly the same things. Don't come back saying that you have retired and it is not within your means!"

"I will … I will."

Granny looked around at everyone and addressed them, "All of you, hear him well and bear witness … he has promised to replace all the jewellery."

By then, Pailen had managed to cut off four of the bangles. Haju relieved the old man of his watch and was taking out the gold buttons on his kurta. In want of a role in the operation, I stood around watching the proceedings. To be honest, I had heard of robberies on trains often enough but never witnessed one first hand. Hence, I dedicated myself to absorbing the entire operation as it was executed.

The old lady hiccupped again and looked at her husband, "Why are you sitting like a fool with the gun at your temple? Take out the buttons yourself. Else, the way this wretch is yanking them out, your old kurta will rip. And if you have some blood pressure pills on you then give me one. My head is reeling. In fact, give me two."

•

AMIDST THIS CONVERSATION, all of a sudden, a commotion erupted. So far, a man had been sleeping on the bench in the middle, wrapped from head to toe in a filthy blanket. Perhaps the fuss broke through his sleep at last. The man pushed the blanket aside and raised his big, round face to gaze around. Red eyes, a bushy moustache hanging from under his nose and dark stubble on his cheeks. After regarding the scene with his red eyes for a while, the man shed the haze of sleep, leapt up into a sitting position and bellowed, "Manke says bravo!"

Till date, I haven't found out the meaning of those words. But the meaningless and monstrous shout perhaps rattled Haju's nerves. Also, he had probably never handled Pailen's pistol before. Hence, revealing himself as the absolute novice that he was, in the use of firearms, he proceeded to make an exhibition of false bravado. Letting go of the old man he turned around and suddenly fired a bullet which hit the ceiling fan with a 'ping'. The man who had shouted out a while back started to jump all over the place shouting louder still, "Killed! Killed!" He was dressed in a pair of khaki shorts and a vest, and his paunch danced to the rhythm of his antics. Pailen turned around swiftly and took the scene in, the dagger still in his hand. Perhaps he took that man to be a policeman. For, nothing drastic enough occurred to make Pailen lose his head and take to his heels. I still haven't understood the reason behind Pailen sudden run for life. Where did he want to run to? After all, it was not possible to run off from a moving train.

He held the dagger aloft and raced aimlessly from one door to another, all the while shouting in a panic-stricken voice, "I'll kill anyone who dares to touch me … I'll kill, I swear … blood will flow like a river, let me warn you…." God knew why he behaved like that! After all, no one attempted to restrain him or hit him. But panic scattered his wits; he stood at the wide door facing the people within, pointed the dagger at them and shelled out one foul curse after another. The two sneering chaps stood by the door, enjoying the breeze. I saw one of them deal a light knock at Pailen's knee which made his balance falter. And immediately, the other chap aimed a hard kick at Pailen's belly. Pailen lost his balance completely and vanished into the sweeping darkness outside.

Haju's rookie hand, holding the pistol, trembled. The old pistol must have had a few loose parts because a screw could be heard rattling away. Without rhyme or reason, Haju fired again. The dark, fat man jumped onto a bench and shouted with all his might, "Bullet! Bullet! I am done for … my belly, my chest!"

I saw the bullet fly out innocently through the window, like a firefly. But who could explain that to the shorts-clad man? He slapped his thighs and screamed away, "Manke says bravo! Another bullet?"

All of a sudden, Haju left the old man alone and dropped to the floor between two benches. Then he started to crawl towards the door, all the while shakily brandishing the pistol at everyone and threatening, "No son of a swine should pull the chain! I still have four bullets left. I can easily kill four of you!"

And then, out of the blue, someone dumped a five-kilo sack of grains on Haju's head. The act proved that crawling was the worst possible move in such a situation. Before Haju could recover from the shock of being flattened by the sack, the young chaps at the door dealt a few well-aimed kicks to his head like professional footballers. From the other end of the carriage, Kadam started to scream, "They have caught me. I'll wipe out their entire clans! Hey Haju, you pimp … fire! Let a few of these drop dead!"

But by that time, Haju was almost unconscious and his pistol had disappeared under a bench. Within a couple of seconds, sounds of heavy thrashing were heard from the other end of the carriage. The passengers had by then collected themselves. The gold button adorned old man also found the strength to walk up to the scene with his silver-handled stick. I heard him say, "Uh-huh … everyone should have a go. Don't crowd around him. Come on, make way … make way…."

And soon enough, we heard the sound of the stick landing on Kadam's head. More people rushed towards that scene while at this end, football kicks rained on Haju's head. A few rustic men squatted by Haju slapping him left and right, and one of them even trapped Haju's chest beneath his knee and thrust a finger up Haju's nostril with the intention to gorge out its contents.

For a while, I stood there rooted like a fool and then abruptly realised that I, too, was part of the gang. I looked around nervously for an escape route.

Just at that instant, the dark, fat man jumped off the bench and enveloped me in a bear hug. He said, "Manke says bravo! Please take a look, mister. Please see where the two bullets have pierced my body. Can you see any blood?"

Greatly discomfited, I said, "Oh no, you have not taken any bullets."

"What are you saying?" The man exclaimed in surprise. "Manke says bravo! No bullets? Huh! But the two bullets …?"

"No, they didn't hit you. I saw for myself."

From the other side, Kadam called out my name a couple of times and then fell silent. The avalanche of blows rendered him incapable of emitting anything but a few groans. At this end, the manhandling of Haju's half-dead being went on uninterrupted.

The dark, fat man inspected himself well and then, assured that the bullets had missed their mark, he looked around and sized up the situation. Perhaps his machismo was suddenly aroused. He took a quick dislike to Haju and said, "What's the use hitting this one? He won't even feel it. Come on, let's go and give some to the bastard at the other end."

And, saying that, he dragged me along. The old man emerged from the crowd, the silver-handled stick in hand, and said, "Oh, how much can my arthritic bones deliver!"

By then, a few of the assaulters had tired. They made space for us and said, "Hit well. Their likes usually don't feel much."

The dark, fat man threw himself on Kadam like a monster. In a flash, he ripped off a fistful of Kadam's hair exclaiming, "Goodness! Is it a wig or what?"

No, it wasn't a wig. I knew. But it wouldn't be to my benefit to reveal that; so, I kept shut. The man nudged me with his elbow, "Go on, give him some! What are you staring at?"

I had no option but to give Kadam some. After all, I needed to keep up the pretence; I feared for my life. I landed two light kicks and dealt a soft slap. Kadam was still in his senses; he looked up once but did not utter a word. Squatted against the wall of the train, he let the blows rain on him. And then, slowly, he stretched out on the floor.

The moment the train pulled into the next station, a ruckus erupted. A massive crowd gathered. I took the opportunity and managed to escape to another carriage. Suddenly I noticed that the dark, fat man had also followed me there. Offering me a bidi he said, "You have done well by fleeing the scene. You are clever. Else, you would have had to get involved with the police."

I grunted assent. Perhaps I was truly clever. No one had realised that I was a part of the robber gang.

In time, I struck up a rapport with the man. Quite an endearing personality he turned out to be. He owned three flour mills in Canning as well as three boats. He took a liking to me as well and finally said, "You seem to be trustworthy. I have three cargo boats serving the area. If you want I could take you on to supervise those. Manke says bravo!"

And, saying that, he broke into a guffaw. Then in a lower voice he added, "My name is Manik … Manik Chandra Saha. I am a *vaishya*, and a *vaishnav* too. I am from eastern Bengal but having lived on this side for so long I have almost forgotten my native dialect. Would you like to come with me? I am a good man."

I agreed readily and set out for Canning. I have found that the wayward always manage to find sustenance, some way or the other. Once one left the nest, there was no dearth of shelters.

THREE

Canning was a nice place. Manik Saha's flour mill was in the congested marketplace. Behind the mill, in three suffocating rooms, lived his three wives. As to the number of his offspring, I lost count. During my stay there, almost every other day I came across a new face among the ones he had sired. Manik himself often floundered when asked about his children. One day, a roadside vendor's son was playing in the mud. Thinking the boy to be one of his brood, Manik dragged him away by the ear and gave him a good thrashing. When alerted to his mistake he clamped down on his tongue, remorsefully, and said, "Manke says bravo!"

Manik Saha was a truly good man. And more than often, he acknowledged the fact himself, "Do you know Upal, I am a good man. People try to scare me by saying that it is illegal to keep more than one wife. It seems, someday I shall have to serve time behind bars. But I say, very well … you can very well send me to prison but don't call me a bad man. I have not behaved indecently with any woman. Lewd men will leave their wives at home and engage in adultery. But I am not like that. Whenever a woman turns my head, I marry her. Now tell me which is the braver deed … this, which I do, or to carry on an affair on the sly?"

Past the crowded marketplace was the wide river, the vast sky and an office building from the British era. Boats loaded with various goods sailed along the Basanti towards Gosaba. Further on, they travelled along narrow rivulets and canals into the depths of the Sunderbans. Spending my days on the boats, I got to know the flow of the tide, the nature of the waters, the clouds and the seasons. Had I not shared in the life on the river, I would have remained oblivious to many of the world's beauties. The area was not served by any other means of transport—no roads, motor vehicles, rickshaws, bicycles or even bullock carts. There were miles of cultivated land interspersed with small villages. Often I moored the boat and walked deep into the land to visit an unknown village. I found a hushed and wondrous world and did not feel like returning.

But Manik Saha turned that life of mine upside down. Once, as our boat left the Basanti and sailed into the main river, a storm descended on us. That time, Manik Saha was travelling himself to look into the trading of hay. The boat was loaded high with hay and Manik, clad in shorts, was seated at the helm humming a silly song, though, I must confess, he had a sense of tune and rhythm. A little while back, noticing a piece of rotting wood floating by like a crocodile, he had shouted in jest, "Crocodile! Crocodile!"

As the wind picked up, some hay flew away like strands of a witch's hair. The sky thundered. The boat groaned. The water darkened and swirling clouds gathered.

Manik Saha turned around and glanced behind with a strange look in his eyes. I was standing a couple of feet behind him and behind me the hay was piled high. But Manik didn't look at me or at the hay. In fact, he did not pay any attention to the tremendous storm that was approaching, casting a dark shadow on the whining waters. He gazed at something else as other boatmen warned us to control the boat.

From atop the pile of hay, Mozammel swung down on a length of rope and said to Manik Saha, "Saha-babu, go down into the hold. If something untoward happens then three ladies will become widows."

But Manik Saha, in his khaki shorts, remained seated as before. Suddenly, the old sail was ripped apart by a gust of wind and it fluttered like a flag. The boat seemed out of control and, being caught in a whirlpool, it refused to gain distance. On the other side, the storm shrouded the area in a hazy veil and advanced with the drone of an airplane. The loose hay blew away in tufts and, after swirling aimlessly for a while, landed on the water. The way Manik Saha sat at the edge, I feared that a strong gust of wind would send him toppling into the water.

I went up to him and grasped his left elbow, then I said to him, "Manik-da, come let us go into the hold and sing some devotional songs."

Manik Saha lifted his face and turned around to look at me. On his left hand he wore five precious astrological gems and two amulets. My grip on his hand disturbed the arrangement. I saw his eyes brimming with tears.

He stretched his arm to clasp my neck with his hand; and then, pulling my head close to his mouth he asked in my ear, "All the work has been spoilt. Isn't that so?"

What the work was and why it had been spoilt was beyond my comprehension. But I realised that for some reason Manik had suddenly slipped into great remorse.

I took a shot in the dark, "Why? Why should it be spoilt? I don't see anything wrong."

But Manik did not utter a word. He remained in his squatting position, the tears flowing down his cheeks and adding to the waters of the Ganga. He simply shook his head from one side to the other.

But there wasn't time for such things. The termite infested mast, with its ripped sail, snapped and disappeared into the water. Nanda's head split and blood gushed forth. In the meanwhile, the boat broke free of the whirlpool and went into a free spin. A few of us took hard tumbles and then regained our footing to find that the world had almost been wiped out. The rough waters of the deep, dark Ganga swelled and swirled. The boat was tossed around on the water.

While everyone was busy trying to exercise some damage control, Manik Saha's shorts-clad frame was stretched out on the deck. The boatmen managed to ram the boat against a mud dam and ground it. Then they jumped off and busied themselves with ropes and posts. But Manik lay still on his back, his limbs flung out. Along with the gusty wind the rain sliced through us. Lightning flashed and struck nearby with a tremendous roar. Manik Saha kept his eyes closed; a few precious stones and amulets had escaped their bindings and scattered around him.

When I shook him, he simply turned over as if he was lying in his own bed. Then he muttered, "All the work is spoilt."

In that region, storms arrived and departed with equal abruptness. When the storm subsided we found that due to the extra weight of the soaked hay the boat had hit the shallow river bed. Moreover, a contrary current was in force. The boatmen quickly tried to offload some bundles of wet hay to ease the weight on the boat. Everyone was soaked to the skin. The hay would be left there and fetched the following day on another boat.

I had a tin suitcase in the hold. From that I fished out a pack of cheap cigarettes and a matchbox and returned to the deck to sit beside Manik Saha. A cool breeze was blowing and the stars twinkled brightly in the clear sky. A drenched Manik sat up and, lighting a cigarette, said, "Upal, I have committed a great offence. Manke says bravo!"

Unable to fathom anything, I asked sternly, "What is the matter?"

He said gravely, "If you had not arrived right then and caught hold of me, by now my corpse would have been floating in the river. Just when my agony had forced me to take the plunge, you arrived...."

His words frightened me. Had Manik Saha really jumped what would my plight have been from the following day? I said, "Why would you jump?"

"The monstrous face of the storm reminded me of my own misdeeds. I have done wrong."

Again the same words.... Yet he did not explain what had gone wrong and how. That night, by the time we reached Canning, the knots in his mind had still not loosened. The days passed. Manik Saha led a normal life – eating, sleeping, conversing, laughing – yet, in the middle of it all, he often heaved a heavy sigh and said, "The act has not been good."

•

WITHIN A MONTH Manik Saha sold off the three boats for peanuts. He transferred the ownership of the flour mill and the shop to his wives. His wives lamented and cursed. But the man remained nonchalant, often repeating, "The act has not been good."

Another few days later, he spilt the beans to me. He said, "Three marriages are not good. Lots of hassles! A single marriage is far better. Moreover, business is meaningless; the real thing is farming."

I nodded like a beat-keeper.

A few days later, one morning, Manik Saha asked me to accompany him as he walked along the dam brushing his teeth with a neem twig. That day too, he was in his khaki shorts with his upper body bare. After a while, he threw the twig into the river and turning towards me, said, "Run!"

Saying that, he broke into a jog; huffing and puffing as he ran. Seeing my sole sustenance in life take to his heels, I too followed on a run. The boat was about to leave when Manik Saha leapt on board. I followed suit.

Then he said with a grin, "That was a timely escape. How can a man with three wives ever have any peace in life? The wives have brought in four brothers to keep an eye on me. Manke says bravo!"

I asked dejectedly, "But where are you off to?"

Manik Saha said curtly, "One marriage and farming. Apart from these I am not going to step into any other trap."

We got off at Gosaba and walked about five miles to the village of Pakhiraloy. There we crossed the river to Dayapur. It was late afternoon by the time we arrived and to my surprise I found that Manik had already set up base there. He had bought land and built a mud hut with a fenced in garden. People worked his fields and there were even a dozen khaki shorts waiting for him.

The very next day, Manik Saha tied the knot. The alliance was fixed sometime back. A dark, young and pretty girl from a poor family smiled shyly as she became Manik Saha's wedded wife. Her name was Jhumur.

Manik said to me aside, "Only one marriage, do you understand? No more multiple marriages for me."

I nodded sagely. Suddenly, Manik seemed to be troubled by his conscience and asked, "Tell me Upal, have I cheated anyone? I have settled everyone's dues, haven't I?" Then he muttered as he counted off on his fingers, "I have not left my wives and children in any financial difficulty … I don't have any outstanding debts with any lenders … I have not cheated any of my employees…."

My life went well in Dayapur. There wasn't much to do except eat well and supervise the farming once in a while. The hunger pang too did not raise its head often. I wondered if it was on a fast.

But Manik Saha's new wife put a wedge in the works. Within a month she started flirting with me. Not that I minded; after all, female company was quite enjoyable and time passed well. But a couple of months later, her hints and gestures grew bolder. Often, late in the night, she arrived at my bedside.

I said, "Look here, for me a shelter is far more necessary than a woman. If you carry on in this way Manik is sure to catch us someday … and then he will throw me out."

In reply, she bragged, "Huh! Is it that easy?" Often she added, "Let's elope."

But I was not that dumb. I tactfully steered clear of such proposals.

Eventually, Jhumur became desperate. The scent of a young and raw male in her vicinity made her shed all pretensions. When Manik Saha returned from the fields and rested, I would say to Jhumur, "Go on, fan him a little and offer him a drink."

But she was always busy falling all over me right under Manik's nose. During the day, disregarding the presence of others, she shot me inviting glances to meet her in the garden.

It would have been unnatural for Manik not to notice. Finally, one day, he roared, "Adulteress! An adulteress!"

Those of dubious character can beg forgiveness at the drop of a hat. And that is exactly what Jhumur did. At first, she fell at Manik's feet, wept copiously and said, "You are mistaken." And then, she accepted her lapse and promised, "This will never happen again."

But old habits die hard! Soon she returned to her ways.

This time, Manik Saha grieved aloud. He begged and pleaded with his wife and tried to make her see reason. Jhumur, too, wept with him and promised again, "I swear in your name, it won't happen again."

But it did. Again.

The third time around, Manik Saha thrashed his wife well and left her tied up in a room for most of the day.

Surprisingly, Manik never told me off on this issue. Only once in a while did he look at me strangely, as if he couldn't quite see clearly through his cataract inflicted eyes. On the rare occasion, he asked me, "Upal, was I better off with the three wives?"

But what did I know? So I remained silent.

He pondered awhile and then said, "The advantage of having three wives is that they are always busy fighting over the single man in their lives … they don't have the time to think about anyone else. Women are a jealous lot! A single marriage is great trouble!"

Lately, Manik Saha had taken to drinking heavily. Jhumur prepared us spicy dishes which Manik and I enjoyed with our drinks as we sat in the moonlit courtyard.

One day, Jhumur handed me half a can of pesticide and said, "Finish the job tonight."

The foolish woman! She was least aware of things like doctors, police, court and the like. Yet, I knew from her expression that if I did not play along then one day the same poison would find its way into my body. She had reached the height of desperation.

So, I mixed the poison with the liquor.

Seeing my preparations, Jhumur said, "What wit! The smell will make him aware that something is wrong. Be sure to get him drunk on the proper stuff first … then have him drink this. That way, in his stupor, he will not find anything amiss."

Jhumur's intelligence astounded me. I wondered how a woman could be both clever and foolish at the same time!

That evening, Jhumur left to visit her parents. She would return the following day all ready to grieve and lament her widowhood! Manik and I settled down with our drinks. The sky was moonless and a lone lantern lit up the courtyard. In the absence of the moon, Manik stared at the lantern sullenly and sipped from the earthen cup. I prodded him with my foot and motioned to him to come closer. As he crawled closer, I said, "Do you understand anything?"

"What about?"

"Listen Manik-da, be careful about what you eat or drink in this house."

"Why?"

"The second pot of liquor is poisoned."

"Poison!"

Suddenly the shorts-clad Manik jumped up and threw his cup away. Then he started to scream, "I have been poisoned! Poisoned! I am dying … oh dear, I am dying! My chest, my belly…."

Shrieking away, he danced around the courtyard in a replay of the scene on the train. I drained my cup and then set off with the lantern in my hand. I had kept a small bundle of belongings ready. By the time I crossed the field and reached the river bank, Manik caught up with me, panting and out of breath. Neither of us spoke. The tide was in. We untied the moored boat, pushed it into the shallow water and jumped on board.

When we reached Pakhiraloy Manik Saha got off into the darkness. I handed him the lantern and saw by its light that his face had a confused look. Behind him, the dark and unfamiliar world stretched to the horizon. He looked in that direction and said, "You know Upal, I have decided to remain a bachelor forever." Saying that, he climbed the steep river bank and disappeared from sight. Till date, I have no clue where he went. I tied up the boat and set off on foot towards Gosaba.

Four

I did not mind living in the veranda. Well, the monsoon and the winter months were difficult but I let such things wash over me.

Every night, the moment the lights went out, a guest graced the veranda with its presence—a corpulent rat. Such glorious health in a rat was a rarity. Almost as big as a tom-cat, the rat rummaged through the utensils stacked below the sink. If I switched on the lights, it went into hiding outside the grilled gate or in a nearby hole. Only its furless naked tail peeked out. It was one sly rat. One night, it shredded and scattered four parathas all over the kitchen floor before making away with another three. The following day, Khawna repeatedly expressed her suspicion, "I doubt this is the work of a rat! I had placed a weight on the lid of the bowl. How could a rat remove that weight? This is the work of a different kind of rat. The kind usually called gluttons!"

The words left me feeling a little humiliated. I felt angry as well, towards the rat.

Sparrows too, created mayhem often. Many of them flew in through the grilled gate and spent the night on the rafters. Through the night, rotund sparrows sat along the edges of the rafters making all kinds of noise. But the real problem was with their droppings. Without a care towards time or decency, they nonchalantly got rid of black and white blobs of excrement. My meagre bedding soon came to carry marks of these droppings. No amount of washing could get rid of the stains. Often, a couple of sparrows sparred with each other noisily.

They pecked at each other and fell off the rafters, tumbling down in a tangled heap.

These were the only two problems I faced in the veranda.

The rat got bolder by the night. The night after it stole the parathas, I switched the lights on as soon as it arrived. We faced each other. And surprisingly, it did not scoot away like it used to. Appearing a tad abashed, it scampered to the grilled gate and started grooming itself at leisure by rubbing its head with its forelegs.

In want of an option, I turned off the lights and went back to bed. I felt a little hurt by its behaviour but the rat did not have the heart to appreciate that.

One day, it chewed up a few shopping bags for no reason at all. Another time, it made holes in a blanket which had been left in the veranda for the maid to wash the following day. Besides, it defecated all over the veranda floor which irritated the maid no end as she was the one who had to clean up. Of late, it was making so much noise at night that my sleep suffered. The lights did chase it away but it soon returned once the lights were out.

One night, Khawna dumped a long stick beside my bed and said, "Don't just enjoy the show put on by the rat! Tonight, make sure you do it in with this stick."

I was in a fix. That night, as soon as the guest arrived, I made a good deal of noise as I got up and switched the lights on. The rat had become quite the maverick. Nowadays, it did not flee upon sighting me. I hit out hard with the stick but it fled with the speed of an Olympian. For Khawna's benefit, I made quite a fuss with the stick and let out some choicest curses before retiring to my bed.

After a few such nights Khawna said, "The rat is getting on my nerves. Get some rat poison from the market today. Nothing else will work."

The order made me break out in a sweat.

The last time I handled poison was to lace Manik Saha's drink with it. Since then, I didn't have much to do with poison. It was true that the world was full of useless people and pests but I quite disliked the idea of using poison at the drop of a hat.

I let a few days pass in deliberate forgetfulness. When the rat raised a ruckus at night, I called out to it, "Hey you fatso, can you hear me? Run away … run away like Manik Saha."

The rat replied with a few squeaks but the communication never progressed further. How could I explain to the dumb creature that it was not wise to trust humans?

I couldn't even kill a mosquito or a bedbug easily. My father too had been similarly inclined. He often said, "Let the little creatures enjoy their short lives"—a line he had memorised from the speech of a learned personality. For him, hitting our pet cat with a slipper a couple of times was the limit; the cruel strain in him stretched to as much. The cat jumped onto the window sill and gazed at my father in wonder. Its eyes conveyed, "You too Brutus?" My father gazed back and asked, "How was that? If you think it didn't hurt, you are wrong. And you will realise that as the hours pass."

I don't know if the cat understood, but, later in the night, my father mixed aspirin in water and forced the cat to have it.

My half-blind Mashi, too, had a generous heart. She invited stray animals and birds to feed them the leftovers. Consequently, not only did a few cats and dogs become her pets but some birds also took a liking to her. Whenever Mashi went out, eleven stray dogs of the area escorted her till the main crossing. When she cooked in the kitchen, the crows sat in the veranda without fear and cawed away in conversation with her. I even heard her reply, "Wait a while dear. Don't be impatient. Sit quietly and I'll make you a few dumplings of rice…."

Growing up amidst such camaraderie, my heart, too, developed a soft spot.

But not everyone's heart was a lump of soft rice like mine. Khawna was without such weaknesses. One morning, while handing me the shopping money, she said, "Why do you make mistakes when you have a list to shop from? If you fail to get the rat poison today then…."

She left the rest unsaid. But it was enough to fill my heart with a selection of unknown fears and misgivings. For an instant, I felt I glimpsed a reflection of Jhumur's expression in Khawna's face.

Khawna had plain looks; she was neither ugly nor a beauty. Her features were all in their right places—her cheeks were neither chubby nor sunken, her teeth neither protruded nor grew inwards. To be honest, I would have nothing to say if someone found her beautiful and at the same time, I would have no reason to protest if she was branded ugly.

As I took the shopping money, I glanced askance at Khawna. Her looks always seemed to change with her circumstances. Today she appeared short-tempered and unappealing.

Subinoy made every effort to avoid going to the market, it didn't tally with his nature. He was a busy man of profound thoughts, quite oblivious to his home and family. His appreciation of domesticity was quite like clicking photographs with a filmless camera. One could go on capturing frames but no photos would come of it. I sensed the lack of such a film within Subinoy. Apart from the work he liked, nothing else in the world could attract his attention successfully.

On my way to the market, I met Subinoy. He was an extremely tall man, about six feet three inches, and rather dark complexioned. Of robust health, he looked quite like a giant. Yet, he was quite unaware of his monstrous strength. Did he even know whether he was handsome or ugly?

Such a tall and broad physique was of no use, just as being too beautiful or too famous was no good. Such people found it very difficult to melt into the crowd or disappear to an unknown destination. All the time, all eyes were trained on them. In this locality, there was a renowned ruffian called Naba. When Naba walked the streets or visited the shops people glanced at him repeatedly, and that was a cause of great discomfiture for him. In this crowded neighbourhood people might well not spare a second glance for each other but they did not fail to acknowledge the towering presence of Subinoy. If Subinoy were to spit or kick at an empty coconut shell or help himself to an unclaimed coin, all eyes would take note.

It was for this reason that I never desired to rise above the average man. Man was often faced with the need to hide or flee and a prominent person found those feats difficult to achieve.

Subinoy held a cigarette between the fingers of his right hand while with his left hand he flicked back his hair repeatedly. It was one of his mannerisms.

We almost bumped into each other and, though he gazed at me with eyes like the lens of a filmless camera, he did not appear to recognise me.

I had walked past him when he called out, "Upal!"

I stopped and turned around.

He looked at me with irritation and asked, "Where are you off to?"

"To the market."

"Market!" Subinoy seemed to ponder over the word for a while. Perhaps he tried to recall where he had heard the word;

he frowned slightly and dwelled on it. Then he said, "But I need you urgently! You will have to go somewhere."

To be honest, I preferred running errands for Subinoy than for anyone else. I said, "Let me get the shopping done."

Subinoy glanced at his watch and said, "No, it will be too late."

"Then?"

Subinoy solved the problem in a jiffy and said, "I'll go to the market. You'd better go to Preeti."

Saying this, Subinoy fished out an envelope from his pocket and handed it to me, "Give this to her."

The envelope had Preeti's address and a stamp on it. Subinoy said, "I was about to post it but thought it would take too long. Better if you hand it to her. Tell her as well...."

"What?"

"Tell her ... Sunday." Subinoy's face appeared glum.

Nowadays, these signs were well within my comprehension. I was doing this for the past year or so. I handed him the shopping bag, list and money. Then I added, "Khawna has asked for some poison to kill rats."

The word 'poison' sent an involuntary shudder through Subinoy. He asked, "What poison?"

"Rat poison. A rat has been wreaking havoc at home."

Subinoy started walking beside me towards the marketplace. His face wore a serious expression as well as a frown. All of a sudden, he said, "My company is foraying into production."

"Of what?"

"Pesticide, insecticide and rat-killer. The most important is the rat-killer. Apparently, rats are spoiling lakhs of tonnes of crops every day. Do you know anything about this?"

"I have heard they are feeding on huge amounts of crops."

"Hmm … lots. The company claims that it will manufacture a poison which will work instantly and also be cheap and easily available. It won't be like the poison we have today … the ones that have to be mixed with dough. The poison has to be palatable to the rats. Else, thousands of tonnes of flour are wasted to make the dough to kill crores of rats."

I was least worried about the crores of rats. Whatever little concern I had was centred on the one familiar rat. I said, "Get the poison ready quickly. Such wastage of crops is not right."

"Work has already started. It is a very important job. If we succeed in manufacturing such a poison then it will be a revolutionary breakthrough. Anyway, don't forget to tell Preeti. Sunday." Subinoy flung a five-rupee note in the air to cover my travelling expenses.

I made swift work of catching the note and said, "Yes, I remember … Sunday."

Subinoy took the road towards the market as I carried on to the bus stop on the main road. I was quite certain that Subinoy would forget to buy the rat poison. It topped the shopping list but would Subinoy pay heed to the list? He was sure to make a mistake.

Subinoy was quite careless about financial matters. A twenty-five-paise stamp was totally wasted on a letter which was being hand delivered. As I stopped at the corner shop to buy cigarettes with the five-rupee note, I wetted my fingers and peeled off the stamp; then I put it into my pocket. Though I had never penned a letter to anyone, who knew when some use might be found for it.

FIVE

Preeti shared a stunning flat with a girlfriend in Golpark. In reality she was a distant sister-in-law of Subinoy's but now she could hardly be called so. They were already way past such formal social recognitions.

I did not know how their relationship came to be so. But this much I could vouch for—Preeti was extremely beautiful. She was fair complexioned and of petite build. A dreamy haze always seemed to surround her, elevating her well above the flesh and blood humans of the world. She had very thick hair which she wore short till her nape. The slightly rough hair framed her doll like face with its big eyes, sharp nose, full lips and a deep cleft in the chin. To be precise, she was well stocked in the beauty department. She had a black birthmark on her left cheek. On anyone else this might have been a blemish but with Preeti it only added to her loveliness.

Preeti had just returned after a four year stint in the US pursuing her doctorate in chemistry.

As far as I knew, till she left for the US she was nothing more than Subinoy's sister-in-law. She often sought academic help from Subinoy. Before leaving for the US she said to him, "I am feeling very scared to travel seven thousand miles on my own! Wish you could have accompanied me."

Subinoy often visited Europe and the US, and spent close to six months there. After Preeti left, within six months Subinoy followed on a US tour. Perhaps that was when their relationship took on a new meaning. It is said that the US is a free country of fun and frolic where nothing need be kept under wraps. Subinoy was never too keen on girls but, who knows, in a foreign land perhaps the beautiful sister-in-law pulled at his heart strings. He returned a very preoccupied and nervous man. Preeti stayed back to pursue her doctorate while at this end the very mention of the US startled Subinoy. For the following months, Subinoy kept the dedicated US postal department on their toes. I'd like to believe that any postman in Massachusetts would, to this day, exclaim in alarm at the mention of Preeti's name, "Preeti again? Gosh!"

At the time, I had just returned from the Sunderbans and was wandering the city streets aimlessly, scouring for a way to borrow some money. I tapped Subinoy a few times and he readily lent me some without a query or a frown, knowing very well that the sum would never be returned. Then one day he said, "Why don't you spend a few days at my place? I have some work with you."

My heart danced on moonbeams. That was exactly what I wanted—to spend my days in unhurried peace in a corner of someone else's household. Like a pet dog or cat, without shouldering any hassles.

I was well aware that I did not have a great role to play on the earth, and neither did I have much to gain from it.

When I first entered Subinoy's household the exchange of letters was already underway. Most of the letters were posted by me. After quite some time, Preeti returned to India and took up a job in a college.

The money that Subinoy handed me towards travelling expenses was much more than necessary. Well, it could be that in want of loose change Subinoy gave me the five-rupee note. But it was a matter of delight for me that whenever I had to deliver a letter or a message to Preeti, Subinoy was always short of change. He always handed me a five- or ten-rupee note and never bothered to ask for the change back.

I had a feeling that the extra money was actually his way of making a request. The crisp note often crackled in my pocket and pleaded, "Don't tell anyone … please don't tell anyone …"

Huh! As if I was going to spill the beans! Why would I? I doubted that anyone would believe me even if I were to tell. People would think, "Upal is a fool … talks nonsense."

I burnt many a candle in mastering this foolish demeanour. I concluded that to get by in this world, one had to be really stupid. Most men were born semi-intelligent. Some spent the better part of their lives trying to achieve complete intelligence while others lazed around and slipped into stupidity. I was always a member of the latter group.

The best attribute of stupid people was that they skimmed over the surface sheen of society and assured themselves that the world was running well. The days dawned, the wind blew, animals and humans busily went about their routine existence, flowers bloomed, the moon shone and men and women thrived in domesticity with their offspring—exactly the way life should be. Their rosy vision made everything appear well and good. These fools never attempted to lift the shroud of normalcy society wore and witness the rot festering within.

Neither did I. Just as the stupid public had no business knowing what the letters and messages between Subinoy and Preeti actually conveyed, I, too, kept myself well aloof.

Sunday. Sunday. Well, my entire life was one long Sunday. While in school and college, the other six days of the week had existed in some sense. In the job of bus conductor, all seven days were working days. And then, an unknown teacher wiped off these working days from the blackboard of my life and chalked the word 'Sunday' on it in bold letters. Every day, I read that word from the blackboard and committed it to memory.

I did not want to dwell much on these Sundays. I'd rather remain an ignorant fool as far as Subinoy and Preeti's Sundays were concerned.

•

THE FRIEND Preeti shared her flat with was called Ruma Majumdar. She was a former member of the women's volleyball team from Howrah. At a time she was known for her lightning speed and tremendous smashes. She used to be called 'Smashing Ruma'. On one occasion she also played for the Bengal team. Once, I had a couple of days off when the bus broke down. At the time, the women's team was practising in Dalmia Park. A few of us rushed there to catch a glimpse of some fair thighs. That was the first time I saw Ruma, dressed in a pair of red shorts and a white T-shirt. Her piercing eyes were fixed on the flying ball, her body coiled in readiness before taking a leap like a cheetah. Then she shot up in a flash and hammered the ball down with a blow. The force of her hit propelled the ball into a hazy flying object before it crashed to the ground and fetched some well-earned points. She was tall, dark and sturdy. She was a good athlete and had won a few swimming competitions on the Ganga. At present, she was a junior officer in government employment and had given up sports except for the occasional swim or a table tennis match. At work, she scared the living daylights out of her juniors.

Though Ruma had a wild look about her and her lean face was slightly masculine, there was nothing scary in her appearance. On the contrary, she was better looking than the average sportswoman. Yet her cold look and crooked smile created a flutter of discomfort in me. Moreover, being a staunch supporter of women's lib, she disliked men with a vengeance. She regarded the love between a man and a woman as animalistic behaviour. Ruma was a staunch smoker needing two to three packs a day. The smoke rings she blew out were perfect.

Even the raffish boys of the neighbourhood refrained from teasing her. Once, a mischievous boy had called her 'Cleopatra' for which Ruma had chased him from Ramkrishna Mission till the railway tracks; the boy, by some special turn of fate, somehow escaped being run down by a train.

Ruma Majumdar was the only reason I felt a little uncomfortable visiting Preeti in the second floor flat. The first day Ruma saw me there, she said in a blood-curdling voice, "I have seen you somewhere! You seem familiar!"

The words left me shrivelling in fear.

Actually, that day at Dalmia Park while the women were busy practising, a few men with not-so-decent intentions had gathered to ogle. They looked well-dressed gentlemen but were of the kind who crowded the Maidan to watch the Anglo-Indian girls play hockey. They cheered and booed the volleyball game with great enthusiasm, as if the future of the nation depended on the outcome of that game. As soon as Ruma's team won the match, the men rushed onto the field and grabbed whichever girl was closest as if to congratulate. One of the men even attempted to steal a kiss or two. Sensing a free-for-all I, too, jumped in to touch a female body without having to shell out a fee. But luck was not with me. The girl closest to me was Ruma, a man-hater of the first order. The instant I shouted "Bravo!" and made ready to hug her, she landed a resounding slap on my cheek. My head smashed to the ground like a ball with my body following close.

Hence, I took care never to acknowledge the fact that we had met before. I always maintained, with an air of non-recognition, "Where would you see me! I am not from Howrah."

Today, Ruma opened the door. She wore a paisley print dressing gown with the top three buttons undone. Underneath, she wore a sports T-shirt whose endurance was being greatly tested by Ruma's tremendous feminine bounty.

I quickly looked to the ground in awe and fear.

Ruma asked indifferently, "What's up?"

Ruma was not privy to Subinoy's letters. All she knew was that I was sent by Preeti's sister to ask after her welfare. But she didn't take too kindly to these frequent visits.

I answered in a low voice, "Khawna sent me."

Ruma said with disinterest, "Of late she is sending you quite often. Come in, Preeti is inside."

Then she disappeared into the flat. Shortly, I heard tango music playing very loudly. Of course I was not sure if it was really tango; for me, all Western music was tango.

Preeti lived in the room at the front. Two of the walls were burdened with bookshelves stuffed to capacity. On one side was a single bed, a table and a swivel chair. Through the half open door of a massive wardrobe, Preeti's huge collection of saris was visible. The floor was covered by a tomato-red rug on which books were scattered haphazardly.

Preeti was bent over the table, engrossed in writing. Recently, she was appointed the head of the department in a college. Preeti had more than enough to spend frivolously, as she was from a wealthy family as well.

I entered to find Preeti's dreamy face turned towards the door. The pen in her hand waited, poised like a dagger. In spite of her beauty, I had noticed that the dark birthmark on her cheek turned red when she was angry. Today, it appeared red.

I couldn't gather enough courage to walk up to her. With a meek smile on my face, I shuffled to the centre of the room and applied my brakes. Preeti seemed quite irritated but I had a job on hand. I took out the letter and, offering it to her, said, "Sunday."

"What about Sunday?" Preeti trapped the pen between her teeth and asked, gazing at me coolly.

"I don't know anymore."

Preeti took the letter from my hand and said, "Both of you are crazy. Tell Subinoy-da, no more Sundays ... in fact, no day of the week. I shall not encourage this anymore."

I repeated, "Please remember, Sunday."

Saying this I quickly retreated to the door. Preeti flapped the letter and called out, "Upalbabu, wait."

I waited. Preeti stood up and came closer. She, too, was wearing a pink dressing gown, but all the buttons were done up. She clasped her hands behind her and stood facing me. Then she said, "You know very well that Subinoy-da's letters are full of nonsense. Don't you?"

"No. I have never read any." I said with trepidation.

"You haven't!" Preeti exclaimed and then appeared to think for a while. "Why haven't you read them?"

"Huh! Is it appropriate to read someone else's letter? Why … does he write rubbish?"

Preeti held out the letter to me and said, "I haven't read this one yet. And neither do I wish to. Why don't you read it? He has gone mad. Soon I will have to take Khawna-di into confidence."

I was flustered. Clearing my throat, I said, "Perhaps this letter is of repentance. Why don't you read it?"

Preeti smiled pitifully and said, "Poor thing!"

"Who?"

"You."

Preeti tore up the letter into shreds and flung them into the waste paper basket. Then she stood before me again. She combed her short hair back with her fingers and held it in place for a while—an extremely endearing gesture. Despite the various anxieties vying for my attention, I couldn't take my eyes off her.

Preeti gazed at me in a pensive manner and said, "Had the letter carried repentance he wouldn't have sent a verbal message about Sunday. Upalbabu, don't you know what that word really means?"

Acting as foolish as I could, I said, "It is the seventh day of the week."

Preeti sighed and said, "Poor thing!"

"Who?"

"You."

"Why?"

"The meaning of that word is not that simple. Subinoy-da wants me to meet him at a special place on Sunday. He has often sent such messages through you … like Curzon Park, evening show at Bijoli Cinema, Saturday Club. Haven't you ever tried to decipher the meaning of these messages?"

"No. But I guessed a little."

"Sit. I'd like to share a few things with you." Preeti returned to her swivel chair and I pulled up a stool.

Preeti twirled around in her chair and faced me. She said, "Subinoy-da's company has given him a beautiful flat in Southend Park. Do you know about it?"

I bowed my head. Unfortunately, I was well aware of the flat; it was I who had decorated the flat according to Subinoy's instructions. Often enough, I met Subinoy in that flat. Preeti didn't notice the play of guilt in my expression. Instead, she said, "The flat is not far from here, about five minutes. Do you know why Subinoy-da did not move to the flat with his family?"

I cleared my throat. The tango music stopped playing in the adjoining room. Ruma appeared in the doorway. She parted the curtains and asked, "Any trouble Preeti?"

Preeti shook her head, "No."

"I'll be in the bathroom," she said and before leaving the room fixed me with a suspicious glare. I averted my glance. Bengali girls were becoming quite dangerous!

Preeti smiled mischievously and said, "Do you know why Ruma plays loud music whenever you visit?"

"No! But I have noticed that she does play music rather loudly."

"She thinks you come here to court me."

My heart did a somersault. And this time I spoke like a real fool, "Of course not!"

"Poor thing!" Preeti said again.

"Who?"

"You!"

This was the third time this dialogue had run. I grew serious.

Preeti said, "Ruma hates the idea of love between a man and a woman. So she plays music loudly when you come to save herself from having to listen to our lovey-dovey talk. Poor thing!"

"Who?"

"Ruma!"

I sighed in relief.

Absent-mindedly Preeti said, "Ruma doesn't know the actual circumstances yet. Had she known that a man wants to leave his wife and children and get married to me, she would have perhaps committed suicide."

I sighed heavily. What else could I do? Till a few days back, Preeti wasn't such a goody-two-shoes. I snitched a few letters she wrote to Subinoy. Even last week, Preeti sent a letter to Subinoy's flat. Subinoy was an idiot—he often left Preeti's letters lying around for all to see. The day Khawna got hold of one, disaster would gatecrash his world. But acting on foresight, I pocketed a few letters as sustenance for a rainy day. My Mashi was keeping them safe for me.

Preeti said, "Yes, about the flat … Subinoy-da would like to set up home there with me. He has even decided to divorce Khawna-di. But till then he would like to spend the Sundays with me in that flat."

I forced myself to appear as abashed as I could.

Preeti said, "Poor thing!"

"Who?"

"Subinoy-da. He pestered me a lot in Massachusetts. And then, after he returned, he wrote me so many letters that I would have had to give up my research work to read through all of them."

I tried to lace my expression with some sympathy. But I knew that Preeti didn't really mean what she was saying; something else was lurking between the lines.

Preeti swivelled back towards her table very slowly. Frowning, she appeared to be lost in thought as she said softly, "Please explain to him, this cannot go on. I am leaving for the US to escape this indecency. I have already received an offer from a place in Minnesota."

Then, before returning to the books on her table, she smiled a little and said, "Why do you act so dumb? Don't tell me you have been unaware of everything! You are Subinoy-da's middleman, you surely know everything."

I stood up and said, "I'll take my leave."

Preeti said, "Yes, and perhaps you won't need to come back here. You aren't a very nice man either, Upalbabu."

I nodded.

Preeti said, "Poor thing!"

"Who?"

"I … myself."

I did not have a proper breakfast, only a couple of biscuits and tea that Khawna offered. Subinoy was on a diet; he was loth to get fat and wanted to preserve his youth and energy. Consequently, Khawna put me on a similar diet as well. But I had no fears regarding my body weight, my youth or my energy level. I just felt hungry. As I did now. While coming down the stairs, the overpowering hunger within me made me want to eat something there and then. These pangs would subside only after I stuffed myself well and for long. My mouth watered and my body tingled.

The remains of the five rupees were still in my pocket. But if I were to sit down in a restaurant that would vanish in an instant; moreover, my belly would hardly be totally satisfied. So pondering I was coming down the stairs when I noticed an aristocratic young man on his way up. He wasn't very tall or sturdy but had a polished look. He was dressed in a pair of denim cargo pants, a cream T-shirt and boots. A pair of large glasses, a prominent wristwatch and a shoulder bag completed the look. It was quite evident that this young man either lived in a foreign country or had just returned from abroad. He was climbing the stairs swiftly as he whistled; on coming face to face with me, he said, "Excuse me," and shifted nearer to the wall. There was a tinge of feminine grace in his face and the distant look in his eyes hinted at his academic disposition. His bag sported the words 'Pan-Am'. I stood there and watched as he reached Preeti's half open door and called out affectionately, "Preeti!"

I quickly made my way down as I did not want Preeti to see me there. A thought came to mind, who would win if someday this young man were to engage in a duel with Subinoy? Subinoy should win unless this youth had any American tricks up his sleeve.

But this was not the time for me to worry about the love lives of the privileged people of this world. The hunger pangs were gaining in strength. I was not so fortunate as to be assured of food whenever I got hungry. Long ago, I had taught myself to suppress hunger. But there were times when hunger made me desperate; at those times, I felt like throwing all conventions aside and just concentrate on finding a way to feed myself.

In the throes of these hunger pangs, I always remembered Mashi.

Six

Through Arpuli Lane, opposite Medical College, one arrived at Madhu Gupta Lane on which stood a big old house. Though a sprawling residence, it was parcelled out among the branches of the family. Much of the portion at the front belonged to Giribabu. The house had a towering main door flanked by porches. The one on the left belonged to Giribabu and the one on the right was his younger brother's. Outsiders were usually restricted to these porches; not many had permission to enter the house itself. Often, when a visitor arrived, Giribabu or his brother would come out to the respective porch to meet the guest. Both the brothers were very fair complexioned and, though not tall, were of stout build. They were in the habit of wearing towels wrapped around their waists with the upper bodies and legs bare. Standing in the porch, each behaved and spoke in quite a royal manner. They could spend hours talking that way and only rarely went as far as to invite the visitor in. If anyone asked why they were in their towels then, for all seasons, their answer was, "I was about to take a shower."

A bluff, no less. I knew for sure that both the brothers liked to be in their towels when at home; they dressed up only when they had to go out. Of course, their towels were well worth praise. They were the best in the market.

At a time, Giribabu showed great skill in the art of flying kites. Now he spent his days tending his pigeons and indulging in games of pasha. His appearance gave an impression of great contentment. Every time we met, he made sure to lecture me on how clear bowels held the key to life's successes.

There was a time when I was restricted to the porches of this house. But now I had access to the inner sanctum. Whatever the occasion, Mashi always managed to get me invited. Since Mashi's entry into this house, I, too, was granted an entry visa. To be honest, the men of this family had many not-so-decent attributes but when they invited someone for a meal, the lavish spread left the guest gaping in awe. But there was a problem—when I would be gorging my way through the maze of delicacies, right beside me the talkative Giribabu and his silent sons would sit timidly after eating a frugal meal. That was the custom of this house. Different arrangements were made for the family and the guests. Moreover, Mashi once warned me in secret, "Don't ask for a second helping. They never prepare extra."

If a list were prepared of the attributes contributing to feminine beauty, then most of the entries could be ticked off for Giribabu's daughter, Ketaki. She was fair, slim and her extremely sweet face made one wonder about the possibility of ants making a beeline for her. She had an air of naïve awe about her. Whoever or whatever she beheld seemed to find a place in her heart. Hence, whoever was the recipient of that illusive glance could well fall under the misconception that she was in love with him. Starting from the milkman to the neighbourhood youths and even myself, all of us often thought along those lines. Ketaki's misleading look was fast eating through society like cancer. On the train, on the bus, whoever looked into her eyes most likely lost the normal rhythm of life. Accordingly, in Kolkata and in the whole of West Bengal, Ketaki's admirers were innumerable. It would need a full-time clerk to keep track of and file all the letters that arrived for Ketaki every day.

But Giribabu did not employ anyone; Ketaki's brothers were ordered to use their idle hours gathering these letters. They looked for and found letters behind the door, at the window, in the mailbox, between the pages of books, in the ventilator grill. Every day, letters tied to pebbles were thrown onto the terrace. In fact, at one point, the ardour of these admirers led Giribabu to almost put a stop to Ketaki's education. But Ketaki's academic excellence made him think better of it. After acquiring her master's degree, Ketaki was now a research scholar of medieval Bengali literature. Two very stockily-built brothers escorted her to and from the university and the library.

Today, Giribabu's brother was standing in his porch. He looked quite fetching in his new red towel as he carefully measured out a few drops of oil onto his right palm from the bottle he held in his left hand. Then he proceeded to massage the oil into his scalp with a vigour that could be matched only by the drive of a shoe-polisher's brush. The men of this family could not speak without raising their voices. On spotting me, Giribabu's brother shouted, "I think I spy Upal!"

He did not suffer from elephantiasis yet his calves were astonishingly bulgy. He followed my gaze and said in the same loud voice, "This is nothing, young man. Had you seen me in my youth your wits would have gone for a toss. My 'muscle dancing' left many celebrities open-mouthed."

I offered him a humble smile and walked into the house. As I entered Giribabu's portion I heard him nearly bringing the house down with his yelling.

"What! You've bought eggs? To hell with those eggs! Go and throw them away. I have been saying since yesterday that I want fish today. How dare you stand their grinning like a jackass after coming home with eggs?"

From where I stood in the courtyard, it was clear that in this house men still ruled. The women did not have much say. Giribabu's wife's feeble interruptions were all but lost amidst his hollering.

It was almost time for Giribabu to leave for work. He stomped his way to the bathroom, the courtyard quaking under his angry footsteps. He noticed me along the irate journey but without breaking his stride, said, "Hey my nephew, Upal! Hope all's well. Now look here … Gobinda has brought in a load of dratted eggs! How can humans survive on bird eggs? Have you ever heard of Bengali blood thriving without a diet of fish? I have told him to throw them into the dustbin."

The bathroom door banged shut. Yet, his raised voice continued to accompany the splash of water from within, "He has pinched money. Find out. I'm sure he has taken to smoking."

By then, his wife's voice had gathered strength in the kitchen, "This boy should be thrashed out of the house. He has gone mad over eggs! Go and return the eggs right away."

Giribabu was still at it from the bathroom, "Search his pockets. He has grown too smart … he has learnt to make good use of money indeed. We, too, pocketed a few stray paise in our time but we never bought eggs in place of fish. Crack those eggs on his head!"

In the kitchen, his wife pushed her vocal cords to the limit and shouted at her son, "If you can't return them then leave this house. I am sitting here all prepared to cook the fish … the man needs to have his meal before leaving for work … and his majesty returns from the market at half past nine with … get out!"

The caustic words chased Giribabu's plump elder son, Gobinda, out of the kitchen and into the courtyard. He looked like a dumb, red turnip. Dressed in a blue shirt and pyjamas, he smiled foolishly as he crossed paths with me on his way out to return the eggs. His looks were perfect proof of his lineage. None of Giribabu's four sons carried any money on them over the exact bus or tram fare. If their slippers suddenly fell apart in the middle of the road, they wouldn't have money to pay for the repair. What to say! They lived in fear that if they carried extra money, they would be sure to spend it. On festival days, when special sweet delicacies were prepared, regular meals were not cooked; the family fed only on those sweet dishes. My father's landlord, who had been displeased upon seeing him going to the market twice, would have been very happy to meet this family.

Amidst all the brouhaha, I did not find any trace of Mashi. But that was to be expected. My simple, half-blind Mashi always considered the people around her as intellectually superior to her. She often said sadly, "I don't know why but whenever I open my mouth I end up saying silly things." And since coming to this house, the fear of uttering something stupid had almost rendered her mute. What little she did say was whispered nervously. She even looked up to the servants of this house with high regard. She never poked her nose into any altercation and accepted both Giribabu's and his wife's opinions with equal loyalty. Whatever she had to say, she saved for my ears.

The blaming and shaming episode was yet to draw to a close. From within the house, Giribabu's wife emerged with a stool in one hand and a rolled up newspaper in the other. She muttered as she approached, "Taken leave of his senses! I reminded him about the fish as he was leaving for the market. He heard very well ..."

From the bathroom, Giribabu cut in, "The fish went in through his ears and morphed into eggs inside his brain! Give him a sound thrashing and throw him out of the house."

My frequent visits to Mashi had won me the status of almost a family member. So my presence did not put Giribabu's wife out. She adjusted the part of her sari covering her head and said, "I'm sure you have already heard the eggs saga! What a lot my sons are! You go in; your Mashi is in the kitchen."

I knew that Mashi spent most of her waking hours in the kitchen. She liked it that way. The world outside the kitchen discomfited her.

Mashi had already chopped and salted the potato and was watching the oil as it heated. Her hand was poised over the cooking pan holding a fistful of finely chopped potato. Today Giribabu would have his rice with fried potato instead of fish.

Hearing me call out to her, Mashi turned her serene face towards me. Tears pooled at the corner of her blind eye and a cluster of stained, protruding teeth stuck out from between her lips. These teeth never allowed her two lips to meet. Her cheek bones stood out and some rough, grey hairs peeked out from under the sari covering her head. Mashi had no looks to her credit and the teeth made matters worse. A couple of my father's well-wishers had said to him, "Why couldn't you spare some more thought before getting married the second time?" Baba replied, "Oh no, had I got myself a beautiful wife, I might have been too smitten with her. What would have happened to Upal? I have married again only for Upal's sake."

Mashi's lack of looks did not bother me the slightest.

As the oil smoked, Mashi forgot to release the potato and said instead, "I have been thinking about you day and night. Upal, do you get enough to eat every day?"

"I do. Why would I worry about food?"

"Come … pull up a stool and sit down."

I sat down and said, "Mashi, the oil is smoking, put the potato in."

The potato spluttered in the hot oil. Mashi gazed at me to her heart's content with her one good eye. Then she said, "I have only the one eye and that, too, is now struck by cataract."

I said casually, "That's quite likely as you age."

Giribabu emerged from the bathroom, sending a tremor through the courtyard. Unable to forget the absence of fish from today's meal, he said, "I'm telling you, he has taken to smoking. Find out. How much did he say he paid for the eggs?"

Saying this, he went upstairs, the old stairs trembling in the wake of his wrath.

Mashi served rice onto a big brass plate which glittered like gold. It was ages since I saw someone prepare a plate of food with so much care and attention. The rice was served in a neat heap in the centre with a tiny bowl of ghee crowning it. Even the salt was arranged tidily. The look of the plate was sure to stir up an appetite.

Mashi said, "The ghee is to make up for the fish. Else, ghee is not supposed to be an everyday affair. Poor Gobinda got a good scolding today."

Mashi's culinary talents were unmatched. In a meagre household like ours, where ingredients were far and few, Mashi had always managed to rustle up dishes which left us licking our fingers clean. She was still as good a cook. Now, as she placed a tidy serving of her vegetable curry on Giribabu's plate, the aroma made me nostalgic.

I asked, "Mashi, do they feed you well?"

Mashi replied in a suppressed voice, "Speak softly. Even walls have ears." Then she added, "They do," and busied herself with frying the potato. She strained the fried potato slivers and heaped them onto the plate adding further to its appeal. Then she asked, "What about you?"

"Of course. A man hardly needs to worry about his meals! Do you have to work very hard?"

Mashi tried to cover up and said, "Not much. I just have to cook the two main meals. But my eye is playing up nowadays. What did you have for breakfast?"

'Tea with biscuits. What about you? Did you eat?"

"I'll eat once Giri leaves for work. I have kept something aside for you. You haven't visited in a long time. Often I wake up in the middle of the night with my heart aching for you … I cry a lot.'

From upstairs, Giribabu's wife called out, "Serve the food."

Mashi got up, the plate in one hand and the bowl of dal in another. Sitting in the empty kitchen, I felt very bad. Had I succeeded in any field, Mashi wouldn't be working as a cook for her square meals. Mashi returned a little later and asked, "Do you run errands for them?"

"Yes."

"Good. Else they will not feed you. I have asked Giri to arrange for your employment in his company."

"Why should he do that? Instead, he will arrange something for his elder son."

"He will do something for you as well. Having a BCom degree is no child's play! Not one of his sons is as educated. And then, you are so talented … music, art, recitation."

Mashi opened an old tin can and took out a few pieces of bread. Handing them to me she said, "Have them."

It was an old habit of hers; she never threw anything away. At home she had even saved the vegetable skins and made tasty dishes out of them.

The bread pieces were hard and crunchy, like biscuits.

"I roasted them by the cooking fire. Aren't they nice?"

"Not bad," I said as I munched on them. "Do they pay you anything?"

"No. What will I do with money? But, once in a while, I feel like buying you a shirt or two. You are dressed so shabbily. Look at the way Gobinda dresses. Why can't you bag a job? Then I could have stayed with you and looked after you."

I had saved about thirty rupees by scouring Subinoy's house for loose change and pocketing some from the money Khawna handed out for shopping. But I did not get the time to bring any of it along today. I took out two rupees from whatever remained of the five Subinoy had given me. Giving it to Mashi, I said, "Keep this. Spend it on something you fancy eating."

Her blind eye was already watering; now the good eye, too, started to well over.

"Bring the rice," Giribabu's wife hollered from the top of the stairs.

"Coming," Mashi answered and hurried away with the bowls.

The kitchen was spanking clean. Not a sign of grime anywhere. The floor wasn't wet and every food item was kept nicely covered. Mashi seemed to have a doctorate in this kind of work.

She returned with a roll of *muga* silk wrapped in newspaper and said, "Get two shirts tailored out of this."

I felt it and found that, though old, it was genuine *muga*. Except for a few scattered water marks, it was in sparkling condition. I asked, "Where did you get this?"

"Their mother passed away a couple of years back. The other day Giri's wife was going through the lady's belongings and she gave this to me. And right away I decided that I would save it for you. Find a good tailor. Isn't it nice?"

"Hmm."

"Ketaki is in trouble with everyone in the family."

"Why?"

"Why else … the girl is very nice but the young men trouble her so much. How is she to blame?"

I kept quiet. Mashi harboured an impossible wish regarding Ketaki—she wanted to see Ketaki as my wife.

I said, "Mashi, don't lose sleep over Ketaki. There are many people here to think about her welfare."

Mashi was peeling boiled potatoes. She said, "I can't help being concerned for everyone. The thoughts arrive uninvited. Through the day, Gobinda getting told-off will be on my mind. He is a timid boy … loves eggs. Often he sneaks in an egg or two and asks me to make him an omelette. I like to indulge him."

Something pricked my heart. There was a time when I reigned supreme over Mashi's heart. Now, a few others were starting to make room for themselves there. But that was to be—I left the fold and what else could Mashi do with her heart full of affection. Fondness was a strange thing; it always managed to find a recipient or two.

I said, "Don't think about Ketaki anymore. You know my situation very well."

In spite of her cataract, Mashi gave me a hard stare and said, "What is wrong? Had you not been lazy, you would have had more than enough to spare. A mother knows her son best. Don't say such things. Now wait while I cook the potatoes; you can have a little with two rotis. Or, would you like some rice?"

"No, no … don't go to so much trouble. They might not like it."

Mashi trained her cataract inflicted eye on me like a searchlight. Just like the searchlight of a ship which found all dangers through the darkness, her gaze, too, saw through the hunger and pain lying within me.

She was a lady of few words. Alongside preparing the potatoes, she served rice in a sparkling brass plate and said, "You are not lucky enough to receive food as well as affection. The people with whom you live must curse you well before giving you anything to eat."

My hunger never seemed to be appeased completely. These days I never experienced the kind of relaxing satiation which followed a hearty meal. The feeling of hunger persisted—now flaming and now simmering. A few days back, one afternoon, Khawna divided a pineapple among everyone—my serving was a little less than what she gave the others. Subinoy, his mother and Khawna chewed the pieces dry and spit out the fibrous remnants. But I couldn't do the same. I gobbled up the entire pieces. I tried to force myself to eat like them for fear that they would think me to be a glutton. But the concept of spitting out the dry remnants never appealed to me. Nowadays, I did not even eat sugarcane that way.

Mashi pushed the plate towards a corner of the kitchen and said, "Start eating. The potatoes will be done soon. Eat your fill; don't be scared."

It was ages since someone said these words to me. They seemed to have vanished from my world. It struck me that perhaps I visited Mashi more to hear these words than for the plate of food.

I moved into the corner and said between mouthfuls, "Mashi, hope you don't get an earful for this."

She raised the lid of the pan of potato curry and the aroma played havoc on my senses. She said, "Don't worry so much. I slog for this family from morning till night. And now if my son has to return with an empty belly then I would be better off on the pavement."

I was surprised by Mashi's fervour. She never had such fire in her. Did the work here make her desperate?

A cat jumped in through the grill at the window; its meow sounded more like, "Ma."

Mashi looked at it and said, "Where have you been? Sit there and wait. I don't know what you are going to eat, there is no fish today."

A crow flew up to the window and perched there. It looked at Mashi and cawed angrily.

Mashi answered, "You wretch! Do you think you can land up at your will? Come back later."

Saying this she mixed some rice and milk for the cat and threw a few pieces of stale bread towards the crow. I wondered if the cat and the crow were the same ones which used to visit our house. Perhaps they had followed Mashi here!

I said, "Mashi, your pets will never leave you. Crows, dogs, cats … and I."

Mashi said, "Ignorant fool."

"Who?"

"You."

"But you happen to be the one who brags the most about my academic qualifications."

"Yet you are an ignoramus. Someone who compares himself to animals is nothing but an ignoramus."

"Yes, I guess I am turning into one gradually."

"God forbid. Just you wait … someday you will be the benefactor of many."

As soon as I tasted the potato curry and rice, the world ceased to exist. My identity and present circumstances melted away. A deep satisfaction filled my belly. I felt as if my heart was without troubles and my mind without desires; all that existed was an impossible hunger.

When I finally returned to reality from that mesmeric state, the world appeared quite new. Through a haze, the kitchen gradually came to life and immediately I found that someone had painted a colourful picture of a girl at the kitchen door. The girl stared at me in amazement. I, too, stared back in wonder.

She said, "Aren't you Upal-da?"

Ketaki looked different, as if she had shed her skin recently. She appeared leaner and rather morose; even her affectionate gaze was absent.

Abashed, I said, "Well … Mashi made me eat."

Ketaki exhaled heavily and said, "From the way you were eating it was quite evident that you were extremely hungry."

I hung my head, guilty as charged, "Yes, I always feel very hungry."

"I don't." Saying this, Ketaki started to ease out the tangles in her freshly washed hair with her fingers. Then she added, "The very idea of eating is very unappealing! I don't feel like eating at all. I don't see how people can enjoy eating."

Mashi sat curled up. A pair of flies staged a duel on her protruding teeth and flew off, but Mashi remained oblivious.

Ketaki leant against the door and flung her hair back. She said, "Your aunt is an excellent cook. Yet I don't feel like eating."

And then she left the kitchen.

Out of the blue, Mashi said, "She is a very good girl. She eats very little and doesn't throw any tantrums."

I said, "Hmm … very nice."

"She is also very intelligent."

"Hmm."

"The boys pester her a lot. But what can she do about it? She hardly pays attention to any of them. Yet, the other day, her mother took the rod to her. The poor girl didn't eat anything for three days since."

I asked in surprise, "How could she beat up her grown up girl?"

"And what a thrashing! With a stick, then with a shoe and finally she banged her head on the floor. It made my heart thump wildly and my body shudder."

"What happened?"

"There is a ruffian boy in the red house at the other end of the lane. He has become very bold, more so because he enjoys the patronage of Giribabu's brother. He is making life very difficult for Ketaki. I don't understand how her uncle can be a party to all this. The other evening, that boy was waiting for Ketaki with a taxi at hand. The moment she stepped out into the lane, he pounced on her with a couple of companions with a mind to drag her into the taxi. There was a great uproar … thankfully they couldn't take her away. And for that, the innocent girl took a beating!"

"Why didn't they hand the boy over to the police?"

"Who could bell the cat? That boy scares the wits out of everyone. Giri stood outside and blustered for a while, then silence descended. After being beaten, Ketaki came to me and wept a lot. She kept asking me to tell her father to get her married off … and free her from this agony."

I asked eagerly, "Did she say who she wanted to marry?"

"No, she is not that kind of a girl. She will marry whoever her parents choose for her. That is why I was saying, had you been somewhat settled …! She is a very nice girl. I fear someday some ruffian will kidnap her."

I sighed heavily and stood up to leave.

Seven

Whenever Subinoy and I had something to discuss we met at his flat in Southend Park. This was the huge apartment which his company had taken on lease. Four spacious bedrooms, a living room, a dining room, a study, three bathrooms, a kitchen with piped gas … and what not? Yet Subinoy, like a fool, was languishing in his ancestral home on Prince Golam Hossein Shah Road. No one in his family knew about this flat.

Subinoy lay sprawled on the sofa in the living room as I recounted the events. He puffed away on his cigarette and appeared quite distant, as if he wasn't paying much attention. But the moment I finished, he sat up with a start. He was in his underpants and vest and the abrupt movement made his muscles ripple. His eyes held a piercing look and he knit his brows in a frown. A seething rage pulsed through his massive body, awaiting release, like a block of dynamite about to go off.

He said, "You have taken my letters to Preeti many times in the past. Has she ever said such things before?"

"No."

"Then why today? Show me how she said those words! Was she kidding?"

"No. She was dead serious."

"I'll be the judge of that. You show me."

Having got an opportunity, after ages, to act out a scene, I launched into it from the point where Ruma opened the main door. As I was settling into the role of Ruma, Subinoy interrupted, "Aah! Show me what Preeti did!"

I felt a bit hurt but jumped into the rendition of Preeti's words and ways. I put up a perfect imitation of Preeti's three different ways of saying, "Poor thing!" I even acted out brilliantly the part where she tore up the letter.

But Subinoy did not seem too interested. Like a spoilsport he got up in the middle of the act and went and stood by the open window. He was not in the right frame of mind to realise how dangerous it could be to stand by an open window in undergarments. Suddenly he turned to look at me and said in a booming voice, "Do you know that Preeti has lied to you? In Massachusetts she used to pester me about getting married. In fact, she had also written to me that once we return to India, we shall get married. But those letters …"

"… are with me", I whispered.

"With you?" Subinoy roared.

I faltered in fear, "Perhaps they are with me."

"So now what?" Subinoy charged to the middle of the room like a wild boar. His almost ceiling-high gigantic frame was throbbing with rage. He asked again, "Now what?"

I said in a restrained voice, "Subinoy, let it be. You have Khawna. Why would you want to get involved in this trouble?"

All of a sudden, Subinoy let out a guffaw. But in the next instant, he sobered up and said, "No genius in this world can survive with a single woman. They need girls. Lots of girls. Do you get that? There was a time when Greek philosophers used to discuss their theories in brothels."

I said timidly, "Since Preeti is not inclined … let her go."

"Don't talk like a fool!"

I was scared, yet I said, "Why do you want to divorce Khawna? She is not at fault."

Subinoy roared again, "So what? Does that mean that I shall have to spend the rest of my life with her? Go and ask all the married men of this world; ninety per cent of them will say that they would like to leave their present wives and marry another girl. And if that is not so then I am ready to eat humble pie!"

In desperation, I said, "Preeti has someone else. He will put a wedge in your plans."

Subinoy marched up to me and grabbed my collar. Then, giving me a shake, he said, "Put a wedge in my plans! Huh! Will he live to do that?"

It was a mild shake but faced with Subinoy's monstrous strength I almost choked. That one shake was enough for me to realise the intensity of this man's physical strength. If ever Subinoy had a showdown with Preeti's male friend I would surely put my money on Subinoy.

He let go of me and returned to his sprawling position on the sofa. Then he lit a cigarette and blew smoke rings towards the ceiling; he said, "Upal, I want that chap face to face."

I said softly, "What is his crime? Does he know about your affair with Preeti?"

"Whatever! I want him before me. I shall ground him to dust in front of Preeti."

This Subinoy was not the tall, decent and well-dressed man people saw walking down the marketplace, lost in his own world of thoughts. This man, in his underpants and vest, was an extremely dangerous lover.

I did not wish to lift the outer apparel of the world and witness the underlying malaises. Yet, life vowed to show me just that.

I asked, "What do you want?"

Subinoy smiled and said, "A showdown. A very practical and effective showdown."

"Will you fight?"

"There is nothing more effective than a fight."

"Subinoy!"

"What?"

"Give it another thought."

"The weak ponder while the strong act. Outside my professional sphere, I am not one to spare much thought over anything. I want Preeti, at any cost."

"If you beat up that boy you may get into trouble with the police, and get dragged into court cases. Perhaps the boy has influential connections. And your career might be ruined."

Subinoy looked up. A yellow light lit up one side of his face, the other side was in darkness. The angular cast of his lean face stood out in the play of light and shade. His gaze was unwavering and his appearance was enough to freeze the blood in the veins.

Subinoy said, "Do I care?"

Then he got up and started to dress. He appeared preoccupied as he muttered, "I believe in simple relationships. I can't stand complexity in relationships." I too, did not believe in complexities. To me, the world was a very ordinary place. The sun rose, the sun set, people went about their tasks, they lived in domesticity with their children, spring followed winter and my belly growled by the ticking hands of the clock. My only problem was my hunger. It was never fully satiated; and even if it was, there was the worry that it would strike back. No Preeti, no Khawna, no lover of Preeti's. Only hunger and perpetual anxiety over recurring hunger.

•

A COUPLE OF DAYS LATER, a man in disguise with dark glasses and false moustache and beard was seen loitering in the neighbourhood of

Golpark and thereabouts. He appeared rather uneasy. He walked around in the morning and evening, stopping for a while, looking up at the sky and sniffing the air for something. His disguise was so unconvincing that a glance was enough to see through it. And his demeanour lacked so much in confidence that any moment the public could catch him out. Often he looked around for something on the ground in front of Preeti's building or leant against the wall gazing at the birds in the sky. Sometimes he stood on the other side of the road eating puffed rice. I knew for certain that if, at that time, someone were to enquire about his identity he would take to his heels like a simpleton or simply break into tears in fear. One evening Ruma found the man sitting on the pavement cleaning his shoe with a kerchief; she frowned at him. And the man, by sheer luck, escaped a coronary attack.

For about three to four days the man roamed the area and kept watch. His skin itched underneath the false beard and the clip of the false moustache pinched the lobe of his nose. Unaccustomed to the dark glasses, he found the area around his eyes sweating. But he stuck to his job—keeping an eye on Preeti and her male friend. Preeti went to college in the morning and returned late in the afternoon. Her friend came once in the morning and again in the evening. He arrived in a red sports car in the morning and often drove Preeti to her college. He came in a different car in the evening and took Preeti out for a spin. He dropped her back home around eight.

The man found out many other things as well. Although Ruma did not play volleyball anymore, she went for a swim every evening in the nearby lake or played table tennis at the YMCA. She was never at home in the evenings. After watching patiently the man also found out about the residents in the flats below Preeti's—one flat was shared by a group of south Indian boys while the other was lived in by a continually squabbling couple who were also fond of going to the cinema. The boys often returned after having dinner outside; hence, their flat was empty most evenings. The other flat upstairs was, at the moment, vacant. Tenants were due to move in next month. The man snooped around and gathered information; for some reason his childish disguise and lack of self-confidence did not give him away. But one day, when a provincial tourist asked him directions to Gariahat, he did jump in surprise and hurry the other way. Another day, two mischievous youths made fun of him. One pointed at the other and said, "Hey, look! Doesn't he look like Habul's father?" And in self-defence the man immediately started to act crazed.

True to his nature, the man spent his days searching for money on the streets. After all, so many people lost money on the streets. All told, he found seventy five paise, a pen, a whole aubergine, a cigarette packet with two cigarettes in it, a lady's handkerchief and a plastic doll. Some of the things were of use to him. The others he saved in anticipation of future use.

This man in disguise was none other than me. Every evening, Subinoy waited in his Southend Park flat for me to report the day's findings. He listened intently and updated his chart of everyone's daily whereabouts. His massive frame, clad only in underpants and vest, gradually took on a killer look.

One day, after considerable calculations, he said, "Upal, the safest time is between half past seven and eight in the evening. Ruma returns around half past eight. Preeti and her lover return between half past seven and eight. The south Indian boys rarely come back before nine and even if a few do return … not a big deal."

Astounded, I said, "What do you mean by that? If the boys are there …"

Subinoy cut in, “I can handle four or five boys by myself. If things start to get out of hand you can chip in.”

“What’s the need?”

“Who said there would be any need! The need will arise only if they return early. Now about the couple, their movements are uncertain. Do they go to the movies on any particular day?”

”Not really. There is no fixed pattern.”

“Unwise of them! Anyway, no need to worry so much.”

“No need to be so relaxed either!”

Subinoy fixed me with a stare and said, “Once I beat up a boy in America because he tried to get up close to Preeti. Nothing happened. Worry fetches nothing.”

I sighed helplessly.

The following day, Subinoy raided Preeti’s flat.

Luck favoured Subinoy. That evening the boys were away and the couple had left for the cinema. Ruma wasn’t in and unfortunately for Preeti and her lover, the couple returned home at half past seven.

Subinoy was waiting in the dark corner below the staircase. I waited across the road. I saw Preeti go up to her flat with her lover. Soon after, Subinoy’s huge frame climbed the stairs stealthily like a cat. I followed.

Subinoy pushed the door open and entered. And according to plan, I followed. I locked the door and stood with my back to it. But I did not have the guts to witness what followed. With my back to the door, I shut my eyes tightly and blocked my ears with my fingers. All I heard were a few muffled sounds. And then, silence.

My eyes hurt from being shut too tightly, my fingers ached and the insides of my ears throbbed. I couldn’t stay that way for long.

So, eventually, I had to open my eyes and ears.

Nothing much had happened. The room wasn't in a mess and none of the items appeared damaged or disturbed. Preeti sat in her swivel chair, her head bent. Her lover lay in a heap at her feet. His glasses lay on the carpet farther away like an injured bird with broken wings. Subinoy stood before Preeti with his hands on his hips, like the lead from a western flick.

It was like a still shot from a foreign movie. Subinoy said, "Preeti honey … darling!"

"Hm …" Preeti responded, as if from a land of dreams.

"Don't you love me?"

Preeti replied in a dreamy voice, "I did. In America."

Subinoy roared, "America? Then let's go back to America where you can love me again."

After thinking for a while, Preeti nodded and said, "Looks like we will have to do exactly that. I cannot love you in this country. Various social norms get in the way."

Subinoy prodded one hand of Preeti's stretched out lover with his booted foot and asked, "Who is this boy, Preeti? What kind of a boy is he?"

Preeti sighed, "He is a coward, a weakling. Just an hour ago I loved him."

"And now?" Subinoy growled.

"Now I don't." Preeti answered softly.

Subinoy laughed out loud like Tarzan, hands still on his hips. It was a wild and naïve laugh.

Preeti didn't laugh. She sat still with her head hung low. Her hair fell about her face and shielded it from view.

The scene appeared foreign to me. As if everything was happening not in Kolkata but in New York or Texas. Had I seen this scene in some movie or read about it in a book? As I pondered, the dormant hunger in my belly made its presence felt.

Really, I was not involved in any matter of the heart. My only worry was this hunger. I wanted to help myself to delicacies at leisure, with all the time in the world.

Subinoy strode up to Preeti. I quickly steered my attention away, unlocked the main door and made my escape from the scene. I flew down the stairs.

At the gate on the ground floor, I met Ruma. A bag hung from her shoulder and she appeared grave as she asked, "What's up?"

I shook my head.

She said, "Did Preeti turn you down?"

Reckoning quickly, I nodded, thinking it would please her. But it did not. With a sulk on her face she said, "Preeti is a fool. She is getting involved with one man after another. Today I shall tell her off."

I said, "Please don't. She is quite sad."

"Why?"

"Her recent affair fell through."

Before Ruma could respond, we heard Subinoy's heavy footsteps down the stairs. Preeti's lover was flung over his left shoulder and hung like a limp bed sheet.

Noticing Ruma, Subinoy flashed a smart smile and said, "He was creating a scene in a drunken state. I am taking him away."

The spectacle in front left the daredevil Ruma quite flustered. She moved closer and grabbed my wrist, "Oh dear! Who is this man?"

I stroked Ruma's wet, dishevelled hair in an effort to calm her down, "Don't be scared. I am here with you."

Ruma almost clung to me. Upon hearing my words she leapt apart saying, "Scoundrel!"

I did not take offence and gave a feeble smile. Subinoy walked up to the car of Preeti's lover. He opened the door, dumped the boy inside and took the wheel himself. Then he called out, "Upal, come on."

Ruma gaped at me in astonishment and said, "You hired the goons, didn't you? You …?" In her anger, the volleyball player of Dalmia Park emerged from within her. With the alertness of a cheetah she fixed her unwavering and sharp glance on me. Then she ran up to me swiftly and raised her right hand which was known for the smash-hit.

But I was better experienced now. I wasn't the dumb spectator anymore. I moved my head backwards as the tips of Ruma's fingers grazed my chin.

I leapt away and began to run fast across the pavement. Ruma gave chase and tried to grab my shirt. In the few seconds it took Subinoy to open the car's door, Ruma managed to scratch my cheek with her nails. She tried to grasp my hand and started to yell with the intention of drawing a crowd, "Thief! Killer! Hooligan! Catch him!"

Subinoy drove off. We abandoned Preeti's lover and his car in a deserted spot by the lake and made homewards.

Eight

The stage was the same—the living room of Subinoy's Southend Park flat. Subinoy was sprawled on the sofa in his undergarments, as usual. He was smoking like a chimney. Soon after returning to the flat, he dialled the phone number he had gleaned from Preeti and informed her lover's family about the exact whereabouts of their unconscious member. Now, he sat relaxed.

The smell of Dettol reached my nostrils from my cheek. I felt slightly weak and my heart was in the grip of fear.

Subinoy sat with one half of his face in light and the other in darkness. Suddenly he looked up at me. It was quite clear to me that he was no longer the Bengali Subinoy; his appearance had donned a foreign garb. Who knew when the change happened!

In a typical American accent he said, "You know something buddy?" I stared at him in alarm.

He laughed to himself and continued, "We are gonna settle in the States. A helluva good country!"

I nodded. The smell of Dettol was gradually fading. My cheek still stung.

Subinoy got up. He opened the cabinet and fished out a bottle of whiskey from which he took a good few swigs. He wiped his mouth with the back of his hand and looked at me with a glint in his eyes, "We were lovers in America. We shall be lovers in America again. You know that buddy?"

I nodded. Yes, I understood. Subinoy gulped down some more whiskey, neat. Then he returned to the sofa and said, "I'll have Preeti, prospects and everything else in the States. That's the country for us. Gimme America buddy, gimme America!"

He smiled a little and then suddenly sat up straight and said, "But there are a couple of important jobs to take care of before I leave."

My hunger pangs were increasing. They were pricking me hard. I slumped in my seat and stared at Subinoy.

He said, "The first one is to divorce Khawna. The second is to invent a palatable poison for the mice of India."

Then he got up and started pacing the room.

"The second work is well in the way. It will be a revolutionary invention. Do you know why?"

"Why?"

Subinoy spoke as if in a stupor, "A very tasty poison. The smell of it will draw out mice in millions from their hiding places … from their holes, from under the cupboards, from the bookshelves, from the pantry. They will feed on it with great relish and then fall into an eternal sleep. Quite like the way the pied piper of Hamlin lured them away. The scampering of mice will cease throughout the country. The only thing left will be heaps of dead mice."

I gaped at Subinoy like an idiot. In my belly, a rat was chewing through my intestines and gnawing holes in my stomach with its sharp teeth.

Subinoy took another swig form the bottle, burped loudly and said, "It'll be a helluva good invention. If I succeed in making the poison, they will award me the Nobel Prize. I shall be the next Indian Nobel laureate. And then off to America. Got the idea, chum? " I nodded.

Subinoy came closer and touched my scratched cheek lightly. It stung. Subinoy tut-tutted with pity and said, "She has scratched you hard. Ha ha…."

Again he laughed like Tarzan and said, "Can I trust you, Upal?"

I sighed, "I don't trust myself, Subinoy. Would it be wise on your part to trust me?"

Subinoy replied dourly, "But there is no one else I can trust with an important work."

I rubbed my cheek and smelt the Dettol on my fingers. Then I asked, "What work?"

Subinoy turned his face away and said, "I spoke to my lawyer the day before yesterday."

"About what?"

"Divorce."

"Oh."

Subinoy blew out a few smoke rings and said, "But it's not easy. I want a clean divorce."

I said with indifference, "File a case."

Not moving a muscle, Subinoy said, "On what ground? Getting a divorce is not easy in this country. Lots of hassles. Moreover, Khawna will not give me a divorce; I know her very well."

"Then?"

"I want a divorce at any cost. The lawyer was saying that if I could get involved in adultery then my wife could present evidence of the same in court and get a divorce quite easily. I laughed at his suggestion. Even if I were to chalk up a hundred cases of adultery, Khawna would never file a case against me. She is a typical woman of this country ... with no self-respect."

"Then?"

"There is a way. If Khawna can be lured into adultery then I can present evidence and file a case."

I stared at Subinoy.

"Do you understand?" Subinoy asked.

I nodded, "Yes. But what do I have to do?"

"You have to play a part in the adultery."

"With?"

Subinoy sat very still and said, "Khawna."

"What are you saying?" I almost shouted in alarm.

Subinoy sat up very slowly. Then he gazed at me for a while and said, "There will be money for it. Enough money."

I shook my head, "That's crazy!"

Subinoy continued to stare at me unwaveringly and said in a grave voice, "Are you a moralist, Upal?"

I said a little hesitantly, "N … no."

Suddenly, Subinoy flung a bundle of notes at me. It struck my knee and fell to the ground. I picked it up and found ten hundred rupee notes—fresh, crisp notes recently withdrawn from The Reserve Bank of India. The staple pins were still in place.

Subinoy said, "Start with a thousand. There will be more."

I shook my head and said, "This is not right, Subinoy."

But my voice quivered.

He said in a desperate tone, "Oblige a friend, buddy. Bring peace to a suffering soul."

I was at a loss. I had already robbed for money and shimmied up to Manik Saha's fourth wife for it. My life did not run on morality. On the contrary, I had this ceaseless hunger. Even when it was satiated, the worry persisted. Like cancer, it never left me in peace.

Like my father, I spent the better part of my life looking for unclaimed money. Not that I did not find any. But we, father and son, never managed to strike a treasure trove or a fountain of gold. Years ago, in the small towns, movies were advertised by a man beating a drum and handing out handbills from a rickshaw. The children ran after the rickshaw and grabbed as many of those handbills as they could. I once dreamt of a man handing out rupee notes instead of handbills from a rickshaw. I have always wished money could be got like that—money obtained without effort or hard work.

I looked at the thousand within reach and smiled. Did I also cry a little as I asked, "Are you really here?"

I forgot about Khawna, Subinoy, Preeti and everyone else. The smell of Dettol no longer reached me and my cheeks did not sting anymore. I just gazed at the money and thought, "You are here! You are so beautiful!"

"Will you do it, Upal?" Subinoy asked and then added, "There will be more such thousands."

I did not know what Subinoy was talking about. I feasted my eyes on the handsome notes to my heart's content and after a while raised my teary eyes to look around me. The room appeared hazy. The man in it was hazy. And light and darkness played in the haze.

I said, "I will."

Nine

At night I found it hard to fall asleep in the uncomfortable packing box bed. Through the square openings in the grill I could see the dark sky. The moon shone and scattered moonbeams fell on me and my bed. I sat up and cupped my hands; they filled with moonlight. Unsolicited yet easily available. This was how I wanted money to come to me. Easy and abundant.

At that very moment, I found my conscience sitting at the foot of the bed. It was dressed like the conscience character from the traditional musical plays—a black robe, full beard, a cap and a fiddle in hand. It wasn't singing though; in fact, it was coughing. It gurgled, "Will it be right, Upal?"

I flared up, "Why? Why won't it be right? Irrespective of my doing it or not, Subinoy will demand a divorce. If he doesn't get a divorce, he might even murder Khawna. Think about it … won't Khawna be better off with a divorce than being murdered?"

"Upal, you are involving yourself in indecency. You are travelling the wrong path. Had you not held the thousand rupees in your hand, you would have realised that this is not right."

I moved closer to my conscience and said, "Listen, my dear conscience, let me tell you the story of Baikuntha, the photographer. Baikuntha roamed around clicking pictures with his old tripod mounted camera. When we were young, he clicked many a photo of ours. Hidden under the black cloth behind the camera, he took so long to focus that we lost patience. But Baikuntha was least bothered, his only concern was a perfect shot. Time and again he left the camera to adjust the positions of his subjects—moving someone to the left, turning another towards the right, telling someone to stretch his hand or asking another to look up. After this prolonged rehearsal when he finally returned to his place behind the camera, I held my breath and waited in anticipation, 'Now, now is the time … now I'll get my photo….' But at the eleventh hour, he always said, 'Uh-huh!' and came back to make some more adjustments. This pattern was repeated quite a few times with him saying 'Uh-huh!' and testing our patience. The moment I readied myself and was almost bursting with excitement, he came out with his 'Uh-huh!' You know, my dear conscience, my fate is somewhat like Baikuntha. Whenever an opportunity arises, whenever I find a way to rake in some cash and dispel the darkness of my life with a ray of hope, someone is sure to say, 'Uh-huh!' from somewhere."

My conscience shook its head vigorously.

I said, "Tell me … why was an innocent lad like me subjected to public thrashing while working as a bus conductor? In Gobinda's house, I agree that I had to flee because of the thieves but what about the robbery? Why did everything go wrong at the first attempt? And then, I was feeding well enough on Manik Saha … but he, too, had to have a change of mind! Throughout the day my belly grumbles and I worry about having enough to eat. Conscience dear, give it a thought … this is the first time I have got so much money in hand. It is like an explosion of wealth, a fountain of riches. Let me do this work. I beg you, please don't mess it up for me."

My conscience sighed heavily and said, "Upal, the money has weakened your resolve. Let me tell you, wealth doesn't necessarily make one rich. The wealthier the person, the more he lacks."

I drew up my conscience by the hand and said, "Look here conscience, do you see these packing boxes? Various chemicals are imported in these but not all of the consignment reaches the company. Much of it is sold in the black market. Subinoy is rolling in money. If some of it comes my way then let it. In fact, it will give Subinoy a chance to do a good deed for a change. Please, dear conscience, leave me alone. Go away."

My conscience disappeared through the closed grilled gate and melted away into the moonlight.

•

IT WAS SUNDAY. D-day.

Today, Subinoy was supposed to take Khawna to the temple at Dakshineshwar. But, as per plan, an urgent work cropped up and he had to pull out. He called me and said, "Upal, you go along with Khawna. I have a meeting with the recently arrived American delegation."

Khawna said, "Let it be, I won't go. We can go next Sunday."

Subinoy looked startled and said, "No, no … you go along. You really want to pay your respects at the temple today … you should carry on. Upal, why don't you shave and get ready?"

Khawna said with a glum face, "I don't understand why busy people get married. This is the only day off in the week … yet, almost every other week you have meetings on this day."

While shaving with Subinoy's expensive razor, I cut myself in a couple of places due to nervousness.

I heard Khawna saying to Subinoy, "Why did you let Upal use your razor?"

"So what?" Subinoy replied, generosity dripping from his voice. "Upal doesn't have any contagious disease. More than that, he is a revered friend of mine. You have no idea how brilliant he was in school and college. A genius in disguise."

Khawna said with irritation, "Of what use is his past status? What matters is how a person lives in the present. Don't let him use your razor again."

Subinoy said excitedly, "You shouldn't say such things, Khawna. With a little effort Upal could have been a celebrated artist or a famous singer or an actor like Shishir Bhaduri. Do you know, he has acted in films? He stirred up quite a rage. But being the bohemian that he is, he didn't want to tie himself down. Even now, he is well capable of achieving a lot if he so wishes."

After shaving, for the first time in my life I got an opportunity to use Subinoy's expensive aftershave lotion. Its fragrance tickled my senses. I would have to buy one of these. Through the day I had thought of many such things to buy! Among them, a safety razor, some trendy clothes, a watch, a radio....

Khawna went for her bath and I used the time to make myself as presentable as I could. Subinoy surveyed me from top to toe and said, "Not bad. But you are on the thinner side. You need a lot of protein and enough carbohydrate. Tomorrow morning, go for a thorough check up with Dr Dutta. Good food and good medicine will make you a handsome man. Remember, you have to beat me in physical attraction."

I smiled feebly and said, "Tarzan, I can never match your amazing height and health."

Subinoy frowned and then said, "Then try to impress her with art or literature or by any damn thing. I don't care. I want quick action."

I nodded.

Subinoy gave me a camera with a self-timer and a tiny super-sensitive tape recorder in a bag. I slung the bag over my shoulder and got into the taxi with Khawna. The children stayed back with their grandmother. Subinoy's seven-year-old daughter, Dolon, made no fuss but his five-year-old son, Ghuptu, threw a tantrum, nagging to let him accompany us. Khawna was keen to take him along but Subinoy intervened.

As soon as the taxi set off, Khawna and I were on our own. My heart thudded with fear and my throat felt parched. My body was as stiff as a block of wood. Khawna, on the other hand, was without any fear and under no kind of pressure. She did not regard me as anyone fit for much besides running the odd errand in her household.

The wind rushed in through the window and blew the free end of Khawna's sari onto my shoulder. Khawna pulled it away and said, "Hope you have worn fresh clothes. It would be inappropriate to enter the temple in unwashed clothes."

Huh! This was supposed to be a romantic rendezvous with Khawna! I felt quite disheartened and said, "My clothes are freshly washed."

Reassured, Khawna settled her handbag, the box of sweets and the packet of flowers between us on the seat.

The taxi raced ahead. The road was not endless; hence, it was time I eased up. If I didn't start a conversation soon I would run out of time.

I stole a furtive glance at Khawna. Neither beautiful, nor ugly, she sat relaxed, gazing out of the window. Khawna paid no attention to me—I was but her travel companion, nothing more. This would have to change.

But before I could say anything, Khawna looked at me and said, "Do you know why he didn't come along?"

Khawna's voice startled me. Not that it should because I spoke to Khawna every day. But at the moment my mind was perhaps too full of her; my heart pounded at her slightest movement.

I said, "He did mention some meeting."

My voice sounded quite flaccid.

Khawna looked at me for a few seconds and said, "I don't understand why he has meetings every day. Why do people call so many meetings?"

I realised that Khawna had thrown an opportunity my way.

I slipped my hand inside the bag and switched the tape recorder on. Then I said, "I agree with you completely on this. I, too, dislike meetings."

I couldn't tell if Khawna took kindly to this similarity in us. She said, "Of course, important people have to attend meetings often. Power brings many hassles."

The taxi left south Kolkata behind and drove on through Chowringhee. The tape recorder was still on.

I asked, "Do you like music?"

"Who doesn't? Why do you ask?"

I sighed, "There was a time when I used to sing."

"Yes, I've heard about it. You were supposedly a good singer."

"I used to paint, too."

Khawna knit her brows and said, "I know about all that. You were a brilliant student. But you couldn't achieve anything."

I took a bold shot, "There is a lot buried in my heart. There is no one to share it with!"

But Khawna wasn't that compassionate. She did not show interest. She said, "What's the use of sharing? Everyone has something or the other buried in their heart. Don't I?"

Glimpsing hope, I asked, "You do?"

"Quite possible."

"Will you share it with me?"

Surprised, Khawna said, "What is the matter with you today?"

The taxi suddenly swerved sharply in an attempt to save an aged widow on the road. I lost balance and banged my head against the door.

"Aah!" Immediately I pretended to be more hurt than I actually was.

"Did it hurt?"

"Badly!"

"Let me see!" Khawna leant forward with an anxious look.

Khawna had no soft spot for me; she felt the sore spot on my head with clinical fingers. But the touch sent lightning shooting through me. Not of love but of fear.

Khawna settled back and said, "Nothing serious. Bathe the spot with some cool water once we reach the temple."

I could have easily steered the conversation towards the pain in my heart and said, "Is the pain only there, Khawna? It is in my heart too." But I dared not be so bold in these initial stages.

At the Dakshineshwar temple, Khawna deposited her shoes and went ahead to pay her respects. I lit a cigarette as I stood on the banks of the Ganga, thinking when I would be done playing around with another man's wife.

Khawna took quite a while inside the temple. By the time she emerged, it was well into the day. She said in a hurry, "Upalbabu, please call a taxi."

I said casually, "Won't you wait awhile by the Ganga?"

"There is no time to gaze at the Ganga. I miss Dolon and Ghuptu. They are not used to staying away from me for long."

"At least, let us visit Panchabati. Won't you feed the monkeys?"

Khawna agreed rather reluctantly. Panchabati was teeming with the Sunday crowd. Children screamed and people shouted. Any effort to sow the seeds of a relationship in these surroundings would be in vain. Yet, to ease the situation, I started walking beside Khawna. What could I say? I couldn't fathom what would make Khawna's heart quiver to life.

All of a sudden, I said, "Would you like to see something?"

"What?"

"I can do a perfect impersonation of a monkey."

"Huh!"

"Really."

I didn't waste any more time. I grabbed Khawna's hand and dragged her to a clearing by the Ganga. Khawna was greatly astonished by my behaviour.

I smiled a little and said, "Don't judge all my actions by human logic. I happen to possess certain ape instincts."

Khawna did not smile. But she did not get angry either. All she did was heave a long sigh.

I stood about five feet from her and imitated the call of a monkey. Then I acted out how a monkey scratched itself, blinked its eyes, groomed its fur, danced around and made faces.

A crowd started to gather around me. The children clapped while the men encouraged me, "Carry on! You're a natural!"

The attention of the public, after ages, felt good. At length, even the monkeys on the trees started to applaud me with their calls. A young chap said, "Dada, they seem to have recognised you … they are calling you."

Drenched with sweat, when I finally dropped the curtain on my act, Khawna was not there. I pushed through the throng of people and started to look for her. But she was not in sight. I felt somewhat confused. Had I acted too silly? Yet, I had to break the ice somehow. Else, why would she pay attention to me?

I walked towards the main road with despair weighing my steps down. A multitude of emotions played tug-of-war within me.

I was walking towards the bus stop, lost in thought, when the door of a taxi opened and someone called, "Upalbabu."

It startled me. I couldn't speak; neither could I look Khawna in the eye. I climbed into the taxi and sat beside her like an obedient servant.

The absence of conversation hung heavy in the air within the taxi. The only sound was that of the engine.

The taxi crossed Shyambazar and sped along Circular Road. Khawna was looking out the window; now she turned her face slowly towards me and asked, "Did your audience enjoy the show?"

I almost died of shame but shook my head and said, "There was no audience."

"What do you mean? You drew quite a tidy crowd!"

I smiled wanly and said, "I wanted but one spectator. But she did not see the show."

"Who?"

"You." And saying that, I switched the tape recorder on slyly.

"Me! Why would I be your spectator? Why were you behaving so disgustingly? Very unappealing!"

I said softly, "Do you know the story of the acrobat? He did shows on the roadside and hadn't any other skill. Once he visited a church and presented his act to Mother Mary. She was extremely pleased. In the same way, I, too, wanted to please you with whatever I have."

"But why would you go to such lengths to please me?"

I sighed and said, "Don't know!"

Khawna smiled a little and said, "Don't do that again. Promise?"

"Okay."

TEN

Today again, Subinoy was sprawled on the living room sofa in his undergarments. The tape recorder played on the table in front of him.

When the tape had run its length, Subinoy blew out smoke rings and said, "Not bad. But if you do not take a more direct approach then it will be slow to mature."

He got up and walked up to the open window. He drained the glass of neat whiskey in a gulp and looked at me, "Look, Upal … don't pretend to be in love. You have to fall in love with her. Seriously."

I sighed and said, "I'll try."

"Hope you remember the assignment for day after tomorrow? At the Metro cinema hall."

I nodded.

•

KHAWNA WAS ASTONISHED to find me take the seat beside her for the quarter past six show at the Metro cinema. She asked, "Where is he?"

I replied apologetically, "Meeting."

"Again! But why did he send you in his place?"

"Else the ticket would have been wasted."

"He could have sold it."

"Well, you do need someone to see you home. When the show gives over, the buses and trams might be very crowded. And, you are scared of taking a taxi by yourself."

Khawna appeared to be bursting with anger and hurt. After a short silence, she said, "I knew he was hard-pressed for time. But I didn't know that he had no time at all."

At such a time, it would be foolish to try and sympathise with her. I allowed her thoughts to dwell on Subinoy. Today too, I carried a shoulder bag with the tape recorder in it. My hand was inside the bag, resting lightly on the switch.

After a while I asked, "Would you like a paan?"

She shook her head. "No."

After some more time I said, "I am hungry. Let me go and get some cashew nuts. The show will begin in a few minutes."

I was walking away when I found Khawna had risen and started walking beside me. She asked, "Can we get tea somewhere outside?"

From her voice I could make out that within that short span of time she had shed some tears. Her voice sounded heavy.

"You'd like to go for tea? Come on."

I settled her in a tea shop and said, "We will have to hurry. There isn't much time left."

She shook her head, "I don't want to watch the film. Don't feel like it."

"Then?"

"You watch it. I'll have tea and then go home."

I stared at her. All my life, I have always failed to complete the tasks assigned to me. Would I fail this time too?

I thought for a while and said, "The buses and trams will be packed right now. Let's sit somewhere or go for a walk and let the busy hour pass."

The waiter arrived to take the order. I asked Khawna, "What will you have with tea? My treat."

Khawna looked at me in wonder and said, "Your treat? Why? Have you got a job?"

"Yes." I replied with a hint of a smile.

"When? I haven't seen you going to work?"

I sighed, "Travelling need not be a part of all jobs. Say, for example, sitting here with you might be my job."

Khawna took my words otherwise and said, "If sitting here with me feels like a job to you then you need not trouble yourself."

Her words were wonderfully romantic. The tape recorder was on alright but I feared that it might not catch the words clearly. The battery was running out. Subinoy had asked me to replace the battery but wanting to hold on to the money for a while longer, I had not yet done so. I wanted to spend as much time as possible in the company of money. These good times would not last forever.

I said eagerly, "What do you mean by job? If my job were to sit with you like this then I wouldn't want to retire."

Khawna did not get angry. She smiled and said, "Of late, you have become a man of words!"

"Words pour forth when the heart blossoms."

This was my penalty shot. Would I score?

Khawna kept her head bowed and asked, "Who has led your heart to blossom?"

"Don't you know?"

"No!"

"Then let it be."

I studied her face with blatant eagerness to find out if I had managed to score a goal.

Early on, seeing us rapt in conversation, the waiter had retreated. Now he returned and I said with irritation, "Two mutton rolls … and tea."

As the waiter left I noticed that Khawna's head was lowered towards the table. She was looking at her hands which lay clasped in her lap.

Goal! Goal! Goal!

My joy knew no bounds. In these mere two days my progress was unbelievable. I felt like rushing to Subinoy's flat right away and pouring out the details before him.

But that was hardly possible. So, I sat tight and chomped on the mutton roll. Khawna seemed reluctant at first but then had half a roll. I helped myself to the other half lying on her plate. Why waste an expensive thing?

Khawna said, "Oh dear, how can you eat from someone else's plate?"

"I don't eat from all and sundry. I am not that desperate. But a particular person's leftovers might be to my liking."

"Oh! You are just too much! You have never come across as so funny before."

"I used to be scared of you."

"Why? What is there to be scared of?"

"I have always been scared of beautiful women."

"Gosh! As if I am a beauty!"

I realised that in spite of the protest, the words appealed to her.

On our way back in the taxi, I let loose many amusing anecdotes. Khawna forgot her disappointment at Subinoy's absence and started to laugh freely.

She said, "Oh dear! I have got stitches in my sides!"

After dropping off Khawna, I reached Subinoy's flat to find him considerably inebriated. He asked, "Something new, buddy?"

I tried to imitate the American accent and said, "Yup."

Subinoy reached for the tape recorder and said, "Helluva good."

After listening to the tape he said, "From tomorrow adopt a more informal approach. There should be more intimacy. The rat poison is almost ready. The visa, too, will be ready soon. Four offers from the States are lying with me for acceptance. Make haste, chum. Where is it tomorrow?"

"The zoo. I'll try to click some photos there."

Subinoy said, slightly worried, "But the children will be there. Dolon and Ghuptu."

"So what? I'll take photos of them as well as us."

"That's a good boy!"

The following day, at the zoo, Khawna and I walked side by side. Dolon and Ghuptu walked ahead holding each other's hand. Khawna looked at the time and said, "Why isn't their father here yet? He said he would come by two."

"He'll come. Khawna, how old are you?"

Khawna smiled a little, "Don't you know it's inappropriate to ask a woman her age?"

Of late, I have gained in cunning and confidence. The right words now graced the tip of my tongue at the right moment.

I donned a mask of seriousness and said, "You look so young that it's hard to believe you are a mother of two."

"Nowadays, you have learnt to compliment very well!" Khawna said with mock annoyance. The glint in her eyes gave away the pretence in her expression.

"Is this a compliment?" I couldn't suppress the eagerness in my voice.

Khawna smiled, "It's common knowledge that such words please women. But my age is not standing still, Upalbabu. Twenty-five running."

I stole a covert glance at Khawna. Unfortunately, she looked well over twenty-five.

Like a very incompetent actor I tried to act extremely surprised and said, "Believe me, you don't look so. You don't look a day over twenty-two. Do you know how old I am?"

I added a good four years to my actual age and said, "Thirty four."

Khawna was surprised, "How is that possible? Your friend is only thirty and you were classmates. You should be of the same age."

I paid no heed to her reasoning and said, "Listen Khawna, you are way younger than me. There is no reason for me to stand on ceremony with you."

Khawna seemed to choke over this. Yet she couldn't disagree, courtesy her sense of civility. So, to get out of the situation she called out to Ghuptu and took a few hasty steps forward.

I gave her time. Lighting a cigarette, I walked on the grass absentmindedly. Dr Dutta had examined me thoroughly and according to him I was in need of various treatments. Belly, chest, eyes—nothing appeared sound. Dr Dutta was a distinguished doctor, with many degrees acquired abroad tailing his name. He was a man of regal demeanour. He took a look at me and said, "Get your blood, urine, stool and sputum tested and then come back to me." It proved to be a great hassle. After going through all the reports he said, "Malnutrition is your main problem." He prescribed various medicines and tonics. I was even taking a course of injections. The medicine further fuelled my appetite; it made me want to sleep more as well. Perhaps I had filled out slightly! And maybe my self-confidence had grown!

After a visit to the aviary, we settled beside the lake. I had already taken a few photos of Khawna and the children. But the most important was pending—a photo of Khawna and me. As evidence.

Dolon and Ghuptu were having a snack. Their faces looked red from the heat and their eyes sparkled with merriment. Khawna looked tired as she sat there and worry was evident on her face. She said, "Upalbabu, he didn't come today either.... These days, he never keeps his word. Why, do you think?"

"He is a busy man...." I said as I gauged the light and tried to adjust the aperture and shutter speed of the camera accordingly—albeit like a complete novice. Then I said to Khawna, "Let me capture this sad face of yours."

Saying this, I set the timer and settled the camera carefully atop the flask some distance away. Once I pressed the shutter, I would have a mere ten seconds to make a dash and settle beside Khawna.

A dilemma caught hold of me. Should I tell her that I was going to sit beside her for the photo? Or should I make it a sudden affair? What if she took offence? What if she moved away at the last instant?

Khawna said in a low voice, "What is the use? I have enough photos."

"I don't." It was true. In my childhood, Baikuntha, the photographer, had clicked one; after that I did not have another photo taken.

Khawna held out her hand and said, "Give me the camera. I'll take one of yours."

I had focused on Khawna with great care and left enough space on her left so that I remained in the frame. There was no reason why I should be out of the frame as the camera was quite some distance away. Yet, I felt nervous.

She was still holding her hand out childishly for the camera. With a smile she said, "Of course, I am a complete novice. You will have to set everything for me; I can only press the shutter button."

Suddenly I had a brainwave. Surely, Khawna did not know about the self-timer on the camera. Khawna was not too wise in the ways of the world. If I were to set the timer, press the shutter and sit beside her then she would perhaps not even notice that a photo had been clicked.

But I felt extremely nervous. Would I be able to pull it off? Would Khawna smell a rat?

Thinking along these lines, I pressed the shutter. The timer started its countdown. I strode to Khawna's side quickly.

But I had miscalculated. Just when I was about to tumble into a sitting position beside Khawna, Dolon ran up with half a piece of cake in her hand and whispered in Khawna's ear, "Ma, I need to go to the toilet."

I heard the click as the timer finished its countdown. Despair!

Khawna took Dolon to the toilet and returned soon enough. In the meanwhile, I had reset the camera.

Khawna sat down in the same place by the bag and snack boxes on the grass. But this time, Ghuptu rushed up and sat in her lap. I felt impatient.

Dolon stood by the water watching the ducks. And soon, Ghuptu joined his sister. Khawna started to pack the bags and said, "Perhaps he is again in a meeting today. Doesn't seem like he will make it. Let's leave."

I gritted my teeth. It was time I took the plunge. Time was running out.

I pressed the shutter with a forceful finger and reached Khawna with two long leaps. Without giving her time to react, I touched my cheek to hers and rested my hand on her shoulder. "Khawna, look!" I said.

Khawna turned to face me with a surprised look and asked, "What?"

"There … a strange bird just flew past!"

Khawna appeared quite put out. I took my hand away and said, "Perhaps the macaw has escaped from the zoo."

Khawna moved away and busied herself with the bags; she said, "What is wrong with you? The things you sometimes do!"

The timer had finished its countdown long ago. I sweated profusely. My hands and feet trembled with excitement.

•

THE FOLLOWING DAY, Subinoy looked at the print. It had been blown up.

"Not bad, chum. You have made progress." He laughed.

The photo had turned out really well. We were captured with great clarity against the backdrop of a bushy palm tree. Our cheeks almost touched and my hand rested on her shoulder. We leaned into each other. An immensely scandalous picture! Yet, absolutely false!

Subinoy was pacing the length of the room with a glass of whiskey in his hand. The hint of a smile played at his lips and he appeared preoccupied. After a while, he stopped and said, "Have you fallen in love with her, buddy?"

I shook my head, "I don't know."

"You look different," Subinoy shrugged.

I sighed. Perhaps I did look different. Had I gained weight? Nowadays I slept well. The worry of hunger did not gnaw at me.

Like the previous day, Subinoy flung five hundred-rupee notes in my direction. "Expenses."

I nodded. I felt a warm flush spread through my body.

Subinoy stood by the window and stared outside. He let out a loud sigh and said, "I don't trust anyone, Upal. And that makes me very lonely."

I did not understand what he meant but nevertheless dwelled on it. I dwelled on it for a long time and eventually got up and let myself out. Subinoy would drink late into the night.

Two days later, Subinoy packed his bags and left for Delhi. Actually, he did not go anywhere. I was the only person who knew that Subinoy would lie low in his Southend Park flat for a few days. He said to me aside, 'Now you will be in a free world. Both of you.'

After a long dry spell, that night the heavens opened. It rained cats and dogs! The rain came in through the grilled gate and I woke up with a start. The heavy clouds thundered like a roaring lion. The torrential rain seemed incessant.

I rolled up my bedding and started to move the packing boxes as far away from the gate as possible. In the process I made some noise. But in the end I could not go to sleep because the spray of rain reached every corner of the veranda.

I lit a cigarette and sat quietly in the dark. There was nothing I could do. I had braved such storms many times in the past. That day, too, I sat like a fool and got drenched.

I heard the door to Subinoy and Khawna's bedroom open. My heart leapt like a frightened rabbit within my rib cage. No reason. It just did.

I saw Khawna's silhouette at the door against the light from within. She looked at the veranda and called cautiously, "Upalbabu!"

I replied feebly, "Hm."

"Where are you?"

"Here."

Khawna switched on the veranda light and looked at me in surprise, "Oh dear! Is the spray coming in?"

I smiled a little and said, "Never mind. The rain will cease soon."

Khawna held out her hand to feel the rain blowing in and then touched my bed and exclaimed, "Oh! The bed is wet!"

I shook my head, "Just a little."

"A little! It is almost soaking! It is not fit to sleep in."

These words had no fitting reply; so I remained silent.

Khawna said lightly, "Your friend's bed is empty. Why don't you sleep there? I'll sleep in my mother-in-law's room."

I shivered, "What's the need?"

"Come on!"

I got up carefully and stepped into the warmth of the well-lit bedroom. I carried my pillow under my arm and also the tape recorder hidden in the shoulder bag. I switched the recorder on. Was this what Subinoy had been hoping for? Had the heavens opened to fulfil his wish?

Khawna said, "He has a very respectable job yet we live in such cramped conditions. Don't know why! How can we manage without an extra room? The children are growing up and friends and relatives visit often. Why do you think he doesn't want to move out of this place?"

"He will," I said tersely.

"Yes, he will … after I die."

Khawna swiftly put up the mosquito net over Subinoy's empty bed. Then she picked up her pillow and a sleeping Ghuptu from her own bed, and said, "I'm leaving Dolon here."

"Very well."

She went into the adjacent room and switched the light on. Then she exchanged a few words with her mother-in-law and came back to this room to arrange some pillows around Dolon. "Dolon is a fitful sleeper. Hope she doesn't fall off."

"Khawna?" I called.

"Yes?"

"Is this necessary? I always sleep in the veranda … through the seasons."

Khawna straightened up and looked at me. Her face was a picture of embarrassment. She said softly, "Am I to blame? Why does your friend live in this small house?"

The house wasn't very small. If they had wanted they could have easily asked me to sleep on the floor in the living room. But they hadn't. And today, I was being courteously offered the bed of the man of the mansion. I laughed, "You mean, you need a bigger house for my benefit?"

"It's not that. Can't you see how everything is crammed into our room? Moreover, the children do not have a proper place to study."

These words were to no purpose. I said, "I shouldn't be staying in this house. It's been too long. Your trials have made me realise that I should move out soon."

Khawna smiled a little, "Please don't be so melodramatic! It's quite late … go to sleep."

"Khawna, I always thought that you couldn't stand the sight of me. I used to think of you as a very haughty woman."

Khawna hesitated slightly and then said, "I, too, had a different opinion of you!"

"What?"

"I thought you were very lazy."

"And now?"

"Now it's different."

"In what way, Khawna?"

"You are a very amusing personality." Khawna laughed. It was a wonderful laugh and she looked very fetching.

"Since when?"

"Since the day you did the monkey act. I was stunned! I

would never have guessed that a timid man like you could actually behave that way!"

"Am I only an amusing man?"

"Very amusing."

I said with a forlorn look, "Does that mean I don't possess a personality to reckon with?"

Khawna yawned and said, "I'll tell you later."

And then she left.

ELEVEN

I hardly trusted anyone in financial matters, neither bank nor post office. My safest haven was Mashi.

The porches of the house in Madhu Gupta Lane were empty today—both the brothers were absent. But four local youths were sitting in the porch belonging to the younger brother.

As I was about to enter the elder brother's part of the house, one of the boys called out to me, "Hey mister, listen."

My mind was already in turmoil over myriad thoughts. Coming on top of that, the unfamiliar call sent a shiver through me.

I took a couple of steps forward and said, "Yes?"

One look at the boy was enough to tell me that he was a veteran sinner. Several gashes marked his face; he was of sturdy build and his eyes were unnaturally bright. His left hand had lost all the fingers. The lone thumb made the left palm look like a cooking spatula. He beckoned me with an imperious wave of that fingerless hand.

As I neared, he asked, "Where are you headed?"

"Giribabu's house."

"How do you know Giribabu?"

"He is my relative."

"In what way?"

I fumbled and it took me some time to recall the exact relationship. I said, "He is a maternal uncle."

Another boy piped in, "Samir, let him go. He comes here once in a while. A relative. Go on dada, go in."

I didn't understand anything. But as soon as I entered the house, a towel clad Giribabu came out from behind the door and dragged me inside. Then he asked, "What did they say?"

"They wanted to know who I was." I asked in surprise, "What has happened?"

"Don't ask, Upal. We are in great trouble. Leaving the house has become a trial and if someone visits then it adds to the trouble."

Saying this, Giribabu disappeared into the bathroom.

The atmosphere in the house was grim. Giribabu's wife was halfway down the stairs when she started at the sight of me, "Who? Who is it …? Oh, Upal … is it?"

I noticed that she looked leaner and her face was glum. After musing awhile, she went back upstairs.

Mashi saw me and her eyes widened. Waves of affection washed over her features.

"Come." The way she said the word implied that she had been waiting for me. As if she was always waiting for me.

I sat down on a stool and asked, "What is the matter, Mashi?"

Mashi sighed, "There is no humanity left in the world! That hooligan boy is making life hell. I fear that eventually Giri and his wife might have to relent and get Ketaki married to him. They are always in the porch. Didn't they catch hold of you?"

"They did."

"They catch everyone. They are guarding the house to prevent us from smuggling Ketaki elsewhere. Giri's brother is with them. The two parties are fighting continuously."

"Where is Ketaki?"

"She is being held a prisoner at home … cries through the day." Mashi sighed again. Then she looked at me with despair in her eyes, "If only you were man enough."

I laughed, "There is no dearth of real men in this world! Don't worry about me so much."

"But that's the only thing I can think of!" Mashi made a pitiful face and continued, "Thoughts of you lead me into thinking about the rest of the world. If only the world were a better place, if there wasn't so much poverty, if men were more generous, then my Upal would not be in such a sorry state. If only everyone understood your hunger!"

I exclaimed in astonishment, "Oh my gosh! You do think a lot!"

"A lot! Do you know, I feed these stray animals thinking of you. I hope that with their blessings luck might favour my Upal."

I sat in gloomy silence for a while.

Mashi said, "She is a very nice girl. And you would have made a nice couple."

"Does the hooligan want to marry her, Mashi?"

"That's what I hear. I think Giri's brother is paying him to make trouble."

The conversation was a waste of time. I took out the money and dropped it into Mashi's lap gingerly. "Keep this safe," I said.

Mashi's good eye almost popped out. She said, "Has an opportunity come your way? Upal … where did you get this?"

I replied with annoyance, "Why do you ask so many questions?"

Mashi lowered her voice to a whisper, "Is this clean money? Hope you haven't taken to unfair means."

"Is that the kind of faith you have in me?"

Mashi slipped the money into the fold of her sari and got up to put it away. Then she came back and whispered, "Ketaki wants to see you."

"Why?"

"Go on. She is in the room below the staircase. Wait a while … Giri has just come out of the bathroom. Let him go upstairs."

A little later, the stairs quaked as Giribabu mounted them. Mashi busied herself with serving his meal. I slipped out and made for the room under the staircase.

Mashi lived in this room. As I parted the curtains I saw Ketaki. She was lying face down on the bed; her hair lay fanned out, covering her face. I didn't have to call her. She must have sensed something; she sat up. It was then that I noticed that her appearance had suffered a lot. In the light that sneaked in through the gaps in the thick window bars, her complexion appeared darker. Incessant crying had left her face swollen.

Without any preamble, Ketaki said in a broken voice, "I want to go away."

I asked in surprise, "Where?"

"Anywhere. Out of this house."

I gazed at the thin girl. She was surrounded by so many hurdles! I said, "Have you planned anything … a destination?"

She shook her head, "No."

"Then?" I fell into a dilemma.

Ketaki's eyes filled up. She gave me a keen look and said, "Do you know what Ma said today? She said that since all the trouble was centred on me, I had better marry that hooligan. Yet, just a few days back, Ma wrongly suspected me and beat me up. I don't want to live here. Will you take me somewhere else?"

Something hit me hard within. Hope burst forth, desire reared its head and my wishes, with their myriad shades, played all around me. But where could I take her? I had no place of my own.

I lowered my head and said, "How is that possible?"

"Why not, Upalda? I don't have time to waste in coyness; else I wouldn't have said this so easily. Listen … I want to marry you."

I was so astounded that I felt dizzy. I gripped the bedpost and steadied myself. After a pause I asked, "Why do you want to marry me, Ketaki?"

This was the most important question and also the most complex.

Ketaki said, "I want to … my wish. Don't you?"

I said softly, "It makes me feel ashamed, Ketaki. I am an insignificant human being."

Despair settled over Ketaki's features. She sat still for quite some time, gazing unseeingly into space.

Then she said softly, "Your Mashi said you would agree."

"The troubled times are misleading your thoughts. When the storm is over you will realise that it would have been a huge mistake."

Ketaki looked away and said, "This is the first time I have said such things in such a shameless manner. Never before have I said these words to anyone."

Saying this, she flung herself face down on the pillow and burst into tears.

I have never indulged in body building; neither was I a daredevil. I was happy to be able to survive in this world by whatever means. What could I do for Ketaki?

As I turned around to leave the room, my conscience blocked my way—the same man in the black robe with a fiddle in his hand. As usual, he spoke in between bouts of coughing, "Did you do the right thing, Upal?"

"What do I know of that? Most people hardly pause to think about the merits of their actions. Not everything is evident to us."

"Still … give it another thought."

"What are you saying, my dear conscience? Do you want that hooligan to beat me to death? And even if I escape with my life, what will I feed my wife? Moreover, the consequences of eloping with a girl won't be any less!"

Right at that moment, my conscience was attacked by a bout of coughing. I took the opportunity to slip away.

As I stepped out onto the road, I noticed that the young ruffians were not in the porch. But Giribabu's brother stood there in his new towel. His face was wreathed in a smile and he called out to me, "Hey, Upal! Haven't seen you around! You have changed … huh? Trendy clothes, polished look. Have you bagged a job?"

He guffawed loudly at his own words.

I said, "How are you?"

"I'm well, quite well." And then, in this heat, he dabbed oil into his navel with a finger while beckoning me closer with the other hand. Then he lowered his voice and asked, "I heard there is some trouble brewing on the other side! Do you know anything?"

I played dumb and said, "I have heard too. Apparently, some hooligan wants to marry Ketaki."

He listened with a serious expression and nodded. "I have heard rumours in the neighbourhood. What a scandal! What does my brother have to say?"

"He is quite flabbergasted."

Giribabu's brother couldn't hide his pleasure at my words. In fact, he almost gave in to a smile. He asked under his breath, "What about Ketaki?"

"Don't know."

He sighed heavily and said, "These things are not in anyone's control! The youth of today … I say, why not make the arrangements and get them married? Nowadays, people are not really bothered about family background and caste. I have heard that in America and Europe such issues have gone for a toss—blacks, Chinese, whites, Hindus … all intermarry without a thought. The same wind is blowing towards our country. Try to explain to my brother that such things don't carry much weight. I know the boy somewhat. He is not bad … just gets into fights now and then."

I said, "I'll tell him."

This time he smiled, "So, you are doing well! I could hardly recognise you! I feel very happy when I see someone prospering. What are you doing these days?"

"The odd thing, here and there."

"Very well, very well. A wave of unemployment has hit us. This porch is mostly occupied by the jobless youth of the neighbourhood. I hardly get to use it. Can't chase them away … where will they go? I am very happy that in these tight times you are doing well."

I managed to escape after some small talk. I was aware that Giribabu's brother was a man of dubious character. He had entered the arena fully prepared to dishonour his elder brother. Moreover, he enjoyed much popularity in the neighbourhood and even ran a local club.

But why blame him? Was I an honest man? In fact, the wisest thing one could do was to refrain from making judgements of right and wrong. I walked along, lost in thought. My heart turned heavier by the minute. Ketaki's words raced towards me like bullets. Again and again, in swarms. They left me riddled. Today could have been a very happy day for me. But it didn't turn out that way. It never did.

At the crossing I ran into Fingerless Samir's accomplice. The boy looked gaunt, with a head of long, rough hair; his Chinese-style moustache hung on either side of his lips. He paid no attention to me.

I stopped and asked, "Can I say something?"

The boy looked at me askance and said, "Shoot."

"A wedding involves lots of problems. Moreover, the girl, too, is not agreeable. Why don't you settle the matter otherwise?"

The boy looked away and said, "Who wants a wedding, mister? Ask them to let the cash flow … we'll come to a settlement."

"Sure?"

"Of course. If some cash comes our way then we'll even help out in Ketaki's wedding. Go and bring her father around."

I quivered in excitement from top to toe. Something ticked in my head. I asked, "Will Samir agree?"

The boy shrugged and replied, "Samir has no dearth of females! Not with the red light area so close. He is toying with them. Ask them to give us two thousand … we'll have a bash, drink away some, enjoy a show or two. But if they don't agree then the matter could take a serious turn. You are close to them … why don't you try?"

"Did you ask Giribabu for money?"

"No. Why should we? Giribabu threatened to set the police on us, so Samir wanted to teach him a lesson. We don't want trouble. To tell the truth, Samir will be worse off with an educated wife from a respectable family … he has studied only till the eighth standard! We have tried to bring him around. He won't listen. But we know that the moment he has the cash in hand, he will relent."

A drum played a merry beat within my head. I asked the boy to wait and hurried back to the house. At the main door, I met Giribabu; he was on his way out. He was surveying the neighbourhood cautiously before stepping out.

He cried, "You are back!"

"Yes, I forgot something."

He sighed in relief, "Oh. Go and get it. I'll walk with you till the main road."

I went in and said to Mashi, "If you would like to save Ketaki then count out five hundred rupees and bring it to me. I don't have time to count."

Mashi was back in a jiffy with the money. I flew out on new-found wings. Giribabu fell into step beside me but couldn't keep up with my near run.

The boy stared at me in awe. I slipped the money into his shirt pocket and said, "The rest next week."

He could hardly believe his eyes and asked in a whisper, "How much?"

"Five hundred."

In a flash, the boy donned a mask of humility and said, "Did Giribabu send this?"

I was an expert in human emotions. In the fraction of a second, I realised that this was the time for me to take the reins of the situation in my hands. If I were to lie to them that Giribabu had sent the money, they would start taking advantage of him. They would trouble him whenever they needed money. I said, "No. This is from me. But if you stir up further trouble, not only will I hold back the rest of the payment but I will also make life very difficult for you."

The boy had just pocketed a bribe; such people were usually of weak personality. Their senses of right and wrong were retarded. He shrugged off his ruffian attitude and said with an indulgent smile, "Why should there be further trouble? We'll take care of Samir. You rest assured."

Giribabu walked past quickly but the boy did not even spare him a glance.

A few of his fellows appeared and surrounded the boy. Perhaps they had noticed the transfer of money. The smell of those notes was like that of roses—those who were addicted to it always smelt it out.

The boy winked at the others and said, "Till next week…."

"Sure. But what about Giribabu's brother?"

The boy said confidently, "He is a fop. We are not going to walk along with him anymore. His son, Santu, is our friend but don't worry … we'll take care of him."

Sufficiently assured, I started off towards the main road. I felt empty within—the money was gone. More would vanish the following week. It seemed as if the money had rained only to flow out.

Giribabu was waiting for the bus with anxiety writ large on his face. Noticing me, he rushed up to ask, "Do you know them?"

"I just got to know them. Don't worry. I've taken care of everything. No one is going to trouble you anymore."

"What do you mean? How?"

Suddenly I wanted to act benevolent. It was ages since I landed such an opportunity. I said, "What use are the details to you? You rest assured that no one will dare bother you again."

Giribabu gazed at me in disbelief. In the past few days, he had aged beyond his years. He released a long pent up sigh and said, "Is this for real, Upal! Do you know hypnotism?"

"I do. In fact, everyone knows hypnotism. Anyway, you had better hurry up and get Ketaki married now."

"To whom? That fingerless Samir?"

"Of course not!" I laughed and added, "I have fixed some screws in that quarter. Now, even if you wanted to get Ketaki married to him, he will take to his heels. I was not talking about him. Find a suitable boy and get your daughter married."

"But what about my brother?"

"He won't utter a word."

"Are you sure?"

"I swear."

Giribabu's mind was almost free of suspicion, but not completely. He dredged up the residue of suspicion and said, "I know of an engineer boy. But they have high demands. Anyway, I suppose this is not the time to worry about such things."

"Finalise it."

"If you say so … Perhaps I can fix a date this month itself. In Kolkata, wedding arrangements can easily be made in a couple of days."

"Do that," I said absentmindedly and walked away. I knew Giribabu's awe-struck gaze followed me for quite a distance.

After ages I felt quite magnanimous.

Twelve

It was drizzling a while ago. I sat quietly on a raincoat spread out on the ground by the lake. The slightly reddish sunlight of late afternoon broke through the clouds. The dull greenery suddenly came alive, as if in a fairy-tale land. The water shimmered. Such was life—a play of sunshine and dark clouds.

I was expecting Khawna. An intimacy had developed between Khawna and me. It ran like an underground stream. Of late, we were meeting outside, away from all eyes.

A new Khawna had been born out of her old self. It was someone who looked at her own reflection in the mirror in a different light. As I was leaving the house, Khawna said, "Wait by the lake. I'll go out on the pretext of going to the cinema. Will meet you at quarter to six."

I flung a pebble into the water. It created ripples. My mind was blank. No thoughts, no memories. The only thing I knew was that Khawna would come. The tape recorder lay hidden in the pocket of the raincoat, waiting expectantly.

It was forty minutes past five. Khawna crossed the paved road in a hurry and stepped onto the grass with a smile on her face. "Hey!"

In a flash, I put on a smiling face and said, "You're here!"

"Am I late?"

"No, not at all." I opened out the raincoat to make room for us both and switched the tape recorder on.

Khawna sat close to me. Our bodies brushed against each other. She said, "The rain started half an hour before I was due to leave. I felt like crying! What if I hadn't made it … you would have waited needlessly!"

Without giving it a thought, I said, "Would the rain have mattered? You had to come…."

Khawna turned her face towards me. Today she had dressed and applied make-up to be conspicuous—heavily done-up kohl-lined eyes, a big round bindi, dangling earrings, a stylish bouffant hairdo and an expensive light green silk sari. Her lips were painted a deep red. The mesmerising gaze of her half-closed eyes dwelled on me for some time.

Then she asked, "How did you know?" A small sigh escaped her. "True. I had to come. Do you know why?"

"Why Khawna?"

Khawna looked at me and said, "Because I love you."

"Really Khawna?"

"How do I explain to you? I think of you all day. Even in sleep you are in my thoughts. The moment I wake up I want to see you. Believe me."

"My state is no better than yours, Khawna. You fill my thoughts, only you."

"Listen …"

"Hmm."

Khawna moved closer. She appeared enthralled. She seemed unaware that it was broad daylight; any acquaintance passing this way could easily have seen us. Of course, that would help rather than cause me any problem. More scandal, more publicity. And more the publicity, the easier things would be for Subinoy. I also knew that Subinoy had posted a few people at the lakes today, as witnesses. I did not know them but they surely would be somewhere around. Watching us. Today, I would have to put on an excellent act.

Khawna brought her mouth very close to my ear and said, "No one besides you has ever found me so beautiful. No one has said to me, 'You are beautiful'."

"You are beautiful Khawna." Saying this I circled her waist lightly with my arm. Then I said, "Not everyone can appreciate beauty."

Khawna sat quietly, perhaps a little preoccupied. Then she said, "Your friend never finds me beautiful. He has never looked at me properly, nor did he ever accept me. Since the time we got married, I have always found him busy with work. We did not go for our honeymoon. We never went for a film or a play. The other day was the first time he wanted to take me to the movies. But eventually, he did not come; he sent you in his place. The same happened at the zoo. Why is he this way?"

I maintained a serious façade and said, "Perhaps great men are like that. In comparison, I am so insignificant."

Khawna shook her head, "No, you are not insignificant. Else how could I love you so much? There is something in you, I can't explain but there is something very beautiful in you. Don't you know?"

I was amazed, "No, I don't!"

Khawna said, "Yes, there is something." Then she grew absentminded again as she continued, "Why did I marry someone so important and so busy? I always hear that he is famous all over the world. It scares me. I don't deserve to be the wife of such a great man. It would be so much better if I were the wife of an ordinary man!"

The afternoon gradually gave way to darkness. Because of the rain earlier, the place was quite deserted. And in the descending darkness and surrounding silence I became aware of some shadowy figures moving around us. Their eyes were on us. Did one of them have a camera with a flashlight? That was part of the plan.

A drizzle sailed over us. Water collected on the leaves; a few big drops fell on us. But I paid no heed. We moved from the grass to a bench and I spread the raincoat over us. Under the raincoat our bodies were sweating in the humid heat.

Khawna sighed, "It is almost time for him to return from Delhi."

I followed with a sigh and asked, "What are you going to do, Khawna?"

"What can I do? At the end of the day I shall have to return to our home."

This made me shiver; I said, "Why Khawna? Can't I take you away from here?"

Khawna shook her head, "That's not possible."

"Why not?"

"My children are quite grown up!"

"So what? Why should you waste your life? Someday Subinoy might land a lucrative job abroad and leave for good. He might never return, he might sever all ties. You would be wise to prepare yourself for that day."

Khawna was holding my hand. She tightened her grip and said, "Have you heard anything of the sort?"

"Yes, I have."

Khawna remained quiet for a long time and then said, "Often I, too, feel that way. I feel as if he belongs to a foreign country and one day he will go far away."

"Khawna, why are you not being more careful? I … I love you."

As I uttered the words, I heard a faint cough. A signal. My heart thumped. I had absolutely no affection for Khawna

… such feelings had never developed. Yet, I would have to complete the task.

Khawna sat close to me. I shrugged off the raincoat to offer a better view. Then, in the shadow of the trees and surrounded by the dark silence, I embraced Khawna. There was no reason for her to object, and she did not. My conscience shied away from the situation. But I could hear it coughing intermittently. It also played on the fiddle to caution me. But I turned a deaf ear. I tried my best to kiss Khawna with as much feeling as possible. But it turned out to be an ordeal. I knew that we were not alone. In fact, Khawna's husband, too, was privy to the scene. The kiss was tasteless. Yet, I glued my lips to hers and waited for the flash from the camera. I waited. An eternity seemed to pass.

And then, a flash. The blue light of the camera almost singed us like a bolt of lightning. Twice in a row.

Startled, Khawna opened her eyes and asked, "What was that?"

"Lightning."

"Oh."

We embraced again. The camera flashlights, in expert hands, went off a few more times.

Suddenly alerted, Khawna stiffened and asked, "Who is shining a torch on us?"

"It's not a torch … just the lightning in the sky."

Khawna gazed at me and sat quietly on in the darkness. Then, all of a sudden, she said, "You know, I think some people are watching us secretly."

The tape in my recorder was running out. I abruptly pulled her close and said, "There's no one. The lakeside is open to all; many people come here to share an intimate moment. Why should anyone watch us? Khawna, will you divorce Subinoy?"

Khawna was rearranging her hair. She appeared flustered and looked around nervously. Quite a dangerous sign, that was. I quickly pulled her closer. She did not resist. In fact, she closed her eyes and said in an almost inaudible voice, "Upal, it has been ages since someone held me close. I thirst for a little affection."

My tape was approaching its end fast. There was hardly any time.

I asked, "Tell me Khawna, will you divorce Subinoy?"

In the same low voice Khawna said, "Do you want me forever?"

"I do."

"Will you love me forever?"

"I will, Khawna. Now tell me that you will go through with the divorce."

"What if he objects? What if he beats you up?"

"He won't. He is scared of me. He will not object."

"Are you sure?"

"Quite."

"Who will my children live with?"

"With us."

"Then I will divorce him."

"Promise?"

"Promise."

I showered kisses on her face and touched her body fleetingly. With the other hand, I covered her eyes and said, "Don't look. Don't look at me."

The camera flashes went off a few more times, from all around us. Shadowy figures moved swiftly from one hiding place to another. The cameras captured perfectly the exact position of my hand on her body.

Khawna said, "Let go. What are you doing?"

I was drenched in sweat. My heart thudded and skidded. Misery robbed my limbs of their ability to move. Inside the pocket of the raincoat, the tape recorder had stopped. The tape had finally run out.

I stood up and said, "Let's go, Khawna."

"Let's sit for a while. I can return later … once it's time for the cinema to get over. It has been an amazing day. I don't want it to end."

My head reeled with shame, fear, fatigue and hesitancy. There was no point in sitting around. It would only add to my burdens.

But I had to sit for some more time, albeit with reluctance.

Khawna said, "You love me a lot … me, Dolon and Ghuptu. My children are naïve."

The reluctance within me stuck in my throat. It threatened to push out like vomit. I had done my bit. The tape was finished and the camera-people had left. Words of love deserted me. I felt kind of empty, meaningless.

•

Late in the evening, Subinoy listened to the tape. Light and darkness played their usual game on the angular planes of his face. Many new lines had appeared on his face. As he listened, often his head lolled. But soon he sat up alert. He seemed restless. After a few drags he snuffed out an almost entire cigarette in the ashtray.

The tape reached its end. Subinoy got up and walked to the cabinet; he took a few swigs of neat whiskey and hiccupped.

Then, very slowly he turned a deadpan face towards me. Uncertainty flickered in his eyes. Perhaps there was a trace of fear as well.

He said very softly, "You know something, buddy? You are a born lady killer! A demon! A dragon!"

I remained silent. A fat bundle of notes took off from Subinoy's direction and landed in my lap.

"Five thousand. You have earned it." Subinoy's voice lacked self-confidence. It was the voice of a timid and frightened man.

I looked down and stared at the money. It was a lot of money. Enough to release me from poverty.

Subinoy stood at the window, gazing outside. He looked away from me and said, "I don't believe it. Yet, the impossible has happened."

I looked up from the money.

Subinoy returned to the sofa and sprawled on it in his usual style. The smoke from his cigarette made him appear hazy. He said, "I always believed that Khawna had glued herself to me. I would never be able to get rid of her. An adamant wife."

He drained half a glass of the whiskey in a gulp and sat in a stupor, eyes shut tight as he tried to absorb the burn of the liquor. Then he looked up and smiled strangely as he said, "You have done it, buddy. Congratulations!"

I got up and had almost reached the door when he called out, "You know something buddy? You are in love with her. Are you going to marry her when I'm gone?"

I shook my head.

"Love her, buddy. Please."

I looked at him. I realised that my eyes were fiery like those of a tiger and anger bubbled up from within my being. But the drunken Subinoy did not notice anything. He said, "I am going home tonight. Wait, buddy … I can take you home."

At night I slept in the veranda again. The packing boxes were somewhat unstable and the bed felt hard and damp. To be honest, I had got used to sleeping in Subinoy's thick, soft bed. I lay awake. Not a sound came from Subinoy's room. Perhaps they were already asleep.

I lay on my side and gazed at the sky. A sliver of the moon shone in the sky. I gazed at it with pleasure. I felt quite disgusted and the moon offered some respite. The moon was of no use to anyone. It hung in the sky without rhyme or reason. Hence, I liked it.

My aged conscience stroked my hair and said, "Sin is like chillies. Hot yet tasty. Isn't that so, Upal?"

"Yes."

"Are you crying?"

"No. I tried to but my eyes don't fill up anymore."

My conscience sighed, "Had you been able to cry, you would have felt better."

"I know. But tears don't come all the time."

Conscience said, "When you have flatulence, it helps to throw up … in the same way, tears too bring relief. Can't you recall something sad? Try … it might get the tears flowing."

"It won't," I shook my head. "After ages, I have seen a task to completion. Now, don't bother me. Please leave."

My conscience left.

Soon, I heard the rat squeak in some corner of the veranda. I sat up, startled. Did the rat not come this way for many days? Or did I fail to notice it earlier? Did my preoccupation keep its calls at bay?

In a flash I remembered that Khawna had herself bought some rat poison today; because I kept on forgetting about it. Before going to bed, she mixed the poison with dough balls and scattered them around the veranda and bathroom. Through the chore, she came to me and whispered, "He is back. But I don't know how I am going to spend another night with him in the same room. What have you done to me? Am I a fallen woman now? Is this right?"

I got up and switched the light on. The rat was scampering over the utensils stacked under the sink. It looked up at me. Its eyes shone brightly. A little away lay a poisoned dough ball. I bent down and scooped it up.

The rat rushed to my feet in extreme greed. It then raised a pitiful face, as if to say, "Give it to me. I am very hungry."

I ignored it. Quickly, I searched the veranda and the bathroom and gathered all the poisoned dough balls. The rat was not afraid of me anymore. It ran between my legs and squeaked from time to time. "Give those to me. I am very hungry. We don't understand philosophy; neither do we understand love, joy and sorrow. All that we feel is an overwhelming hunger."

I knelt down and faced the rat. I said, "Am I not like you? But you shouldn't eat all that you happen to find. Someone has scattered many such poisoned titbits around me. Once in a while I help myself to them. They cause a lot of pain."

THIRTEEN

Subinoy left for work. Khawna went shopping. Subinoy's mother went to the Kalighat temple with the maid, Kusum.

I was in the bathroom, intently washing my vest. Of late, Khawna expressed displeasure when she found me washing clothes, "Why should you wash clothes? Kusum will do it. Else, I'll do it. Men are hardly made for such chores!"

It was not that I was keen on washing vests. But I thought, I'd have to do it for the rest of my life ... there was no other way. After all, I would never have a wife. Instead, I would have to pay off the hooligans of Madhu Gupta Lane from my own pocket. Ketaki's wedding date had been finalised. The groom—the same engineer boy. So was this indulgent offer of personal service any good after so many years, I thought to myself. Why should I accept it? My life would find a way.

Someone arrived at the bathroom door. At first I did not look up. But then, realising that someone was standing still as a statue, I had to raise my eyes. And I was greatly astonished.

"Preeti!" My voice quivered.

She wore a very expensive white sari with a wide gold border. Her face was pale and her lips drained of colour. She looked very morose.

She took a few steps forward and said, "I have come to see you."

"Me?"

"Upalbabu, you messed up Khawna-di?"

I looked down and said, "Certainly not. I love her."

Preeti flopped down on the dirty and wet threshold of the bathroom, quite oblivious of her expensive sari. She locked her gaze with mine and stared hard into my eyes.

"What?" I asked in surprise.

"I know everything, Upalbabu."

I lowered my head again and said, "I swear …"

"Poor thing!" Preeti laughed. "No, not Khawna-di … but you. You love money too much."

I shook my head, "No. I don't love money. I only wanted money to be easily available! I wanted it to rain down freely. I wished it to be distributed freely like handbills at every crossing."

"So you went ahead and shamed my cousin for money?"

"Shamed?" I asked, astonished. Then I crawled closer to Preeti and pushed my face towards hers. She jumped up; perhaps she thought I had gone mad.

"I have not brought shame on anyone. Each person bears the fruit of his own karma. I am insignificant."

Preeti looked at me with repugnance in her eyes, the way people glanced at a dead rat by the roadside. After a while she said, "Don't you wish to go somewhere else?" I washed the vest and wrung out the water. Then I got up and said, "I will. I will have to go. Preeti, this is the first time in my life that I have completed a task. Please let me revel in that feeling for some time."

"What task?"

"I have removed Khawna from your path. Now, the two of you can leave for America."

"Poor thing!" Preeti's sigh echoed through the room. She said, "Do you think I will trust the man who has gone to such lengths to scandalise his wife? I have known Khawna-di since we were children. She was always a very homely person. The way she played with her dolls made others comment favourably on her future as a perfect homemaker. And Khawna-di turned out exactly that way. Her world revolves around her husband, children, mother-in-law and her home. What kind of a man drags such a perfect wife into filth?"

I nodded in agreement.

Preeti put her hand on mine and said, "Why did you do it? How did you turn her head?"

I replied in a sad voice, "I am insignificant. What happened was predestined."

Preeti took a step closer and said, "Nothing has happened, Upalbabu. I have never given Subinoy-da a place in my heart. Perhaps there have been weak moments, but not anymore. I have come to take you away."

"Where, Preeti?"

"I need you urgently."

"Why, Preeti?"

"I'll tell you. Please pack your stuff."

"There is nothing much to pack."

"Then let's go."

I got dressed and pocketed the thick bundle of notes.

Preeti looked at it askance and exclaimed, "How much!"

"Lots!"

Preeti looked at me with pity in her eyes.

She had kept the taxi waiting. As I got in, I was stunned to see Ruma sitting inside. She was sitting comfortably in the rear seat and examining the nails of her left hand. She shot me a sharp glance and said to Preeti, "Have you explained everything to him?"

"No, you tell him."

"Alright." Ruma sat in the middle with Preeti and me on either side.

The taxi started and drove on leisurely. Perhaps the driver was instructed to do so.

Ruma's proximity made my body stiffen. Fear lurked in my heart and I felt quite nervous.

She brought her mouth close to my ear and said, "Listen Romeo, Preeti has at last agreed to marry you." I gulped a large mouthful of air.

"Me?"

"Yes, you. Why, aren't you willing?"

I answered frantically, "What are you saying? Did I hear right?"

"Yes, you did. Preeti wants to marry you. Today, right now. She has chosen you from amongst many suitors. You are a lucky man."

My head swam. I couldn't comprehend anything. I stared blankly at the green turban of the Punjabi taxi driver. My body seemed to be in contact with a live electric wire. A shock ran through me from time to time making my body tremble. I turned towards Preeti and looked at her anew.

Preeti was looking at me; as our eyes met, she turned away to look out of the window.

We reached their flat in Golpark. Ruma said, "I am in the other room. You two have a good talk."

Ruma went into her room and locked the door. Soon tango music floated out from her room.

Preeti sat in her swivel chair, her head bent low. Her short curls framed her face like bunches of dark grapes.

I sat on a cushioned stool, flabbergasted. Words deserted me.

After a long while, Preeti raised her pretty yet pale face and looked at me. She called in a soft and affectionate voice, "Upal!"

"Hm."

"Won't you marry me, Upal?"

I said, "Am I dreaming, Preeti?"

"No," Preeti shook her head. "Upal, I can't do without you."

I rubbed my eyes, trying to clear my thoughts, and said, "No one loves me, Preeti."

Preeti again lowered her head and said from behind the dark curls, "I do."

"Since when, Preeti?"

"The day I first met you … when you delivered Subinoyda's crazy letter to me. I was annoyed with you but I couldn't forget you. I tried to find the reason why and felt irritated with myself. Later, I realised that at some point of time I had fallen in love with you. It had angered me. But love is beyond one's control! Right?"

"Preeti, I am a very ordinary man."

"Who said? You are not ordinary. You have never realised your potential."

"What is it, Preeti?"

"You are a very good man. You are very nice."

I shook my head, "No, Preeti. I am not good. When I am hungry, I take leave of my senses. And then I do whatever I am asked to do. I have always got the short end of the stick. If only I did not feel hungry …"

Preeti looked at me with wide eyes brimming with tears. Her lips quivered. She seemed at a loss for words. Then she said in a changed voice, "I will feed you, Upal. I'll take you to America. We'll work together, earn and eat together. Don't talk about hunger. It makes me feel very sad."

Astonished, I said, "You will take me to America?"

She nodded, "Yes, I will. I am leaving this Sunday. I'll make arrangements for you to join me as soon as I reach America. Don't worry, there is no shortage of food in that country."

"You'll take me!" Tango music flowed through my veins. A dance floor spread out within me and fair skinned couples twirled on it.

"Preeti!"

Preeti had her ears trained elsewhere. She said, "Hmm…."

"When are we getting married?"

"Today. The marriage registrar and witnesses will arrive at three in the afternoon."

I laughed. It was ages since I last laughed this way, like a fool.

"Preeti, after the wedding we'll visit Mashi."

Preeti asked in surprise, "Who is Mashi?"

"I have an aunt. She is the only person I have in this world. She will be very happy and will shower you with love. Won't you come with me?"

"Of course, Upal!"

"Will you touch her feet with respect?'

"Of course."

"What is the time, Preeti?"

She smiled a little and said, "Five minutes to three. I hope you are not nervous."

I stared at her, surprised, and said, "No! Why should I be nervous? I am bursting with joy. Preeti, after the wedding will you put sindoor in the parting of your hair?"

She raised a sorry face and said, "I will have to."

"Can you cook, Preeti dear?"

Preeti tilted her head and said, "Yes. I can cook various dishes … native and foreign. In America, I will have to cook for you."

"Why Preeti? We will hire a cook."

"Such services are very expensive in that country."

"I don't care. I won't let you cook."

"Very well", Preeti smiled a little.

We heard footsteps on the stairs. I stood up in excitement.

Preeti stood up as well. With a pale face she said, "They are here."

I ran a palm over my cheeks and said, "I haven't shaved today, Preeti."

"Never mind. You will be doing that for the rest of your life."

"I don't have nice clothes on."

"I'll buy you many nice clothes."

Three men entered the room. One of them carried some papers. In my excitement, I did not look at them properly at first but then I realised that one of them was Preeti's lover.

Preeti moved closer to me. And one of her hands crept into mine. I whispered to her, "Who is he, Preeti? Why is he here?"

Preeti replied softly, "He is no one. He is here only as a witness."

The tango music stopped and Ruma emerged from her room. The man with the papers settled himself in a chair at the table. Preeti's ex-lover and another unfamiliar man remained standing with grave expressions.

The atmosphere in the room was heavy. No one expressed any joy. How could a marriage be solemnised in such gloomy surroundings?

Preeti gripped my hand and said, "Come, Upal."

I said, "Preeti, no one seems bothered about the rituals.—no blowing of conch shells …"

Preeti led me to the table. The marriage registrar pointed to a place on the form and said, "Sign here."

It took no time at all. After Preeti and I had signed Ruma, Preeti's ex-lover and the unfamiliar man signed too. The marriage registrar packed his paraphernalia and left.

Preeti sat down in her swivel chair, head bent low. Her face was framed by her hair hanging like bunches of black grapes. All of a sudden she shuddered and the muffled sound of suppressed tears floated up to me. As I made to rush towards her from the middle of the room, Ruma barred my way.

"Upalbabu, please don't disturb her now!"

"Disturb!" I exclaimed. "What do you mean? She is my wife! I need to find out why my wife is crying."

Preeti's ex-lover and the other man flanked Ruma on either side. The ex-lover looked at me with doleful eyes and said, "You are right, of course. She is now yours forever. Please let her rest for a while."

I said anxiously, "Please let me go to her. My wife is crying…"

Ruma said in a pensive voice, "Upalbabu, as of now, she is your wife only on paper. And you should be satisfied with that."

Astonished, I said, "Wife on paper! What do you mean?"

"A wife by virtue of signing on the dotted line." Then Ruma added in a harsh voice, "Nothing more."

I gaped like a fool. The three of them stood like a wall before me. On the other side of this wall Preeti sobbed uncontrollably, her head resting on the table.

"Preeti!" I called out to her from the very depths of my heart.

But she did not reply. Neither did she stop sobbing.

The ex-lover took my hand in his and said, "Don't get emotional, Upalbabu. You have many responsibilities now."

I nodded, "Of course. Marriage brings responsibilities."

He nodded too and said, "That is what I am saying, there is much to be done. The first thing for you to do is to reach the news to Subinoy. Inform him that you and Preeti are now married. This is very important, Upalbabu."

I could not fathom much. Everything appeared murky. Yet I nodded. Through my life, people have ordered me to run various errands, some right and some wrong. I have always carried them out.

The ex-lover said, "Do you know why it is important? Subinoy's eccentric behaviour has peaked. He has been watching Preeti constantly. But Preeti has to fly the day after tomorrow."

"Day after!" I exclaimed.

'Yes, day after … Sunday. Her tickets are booked."

I asked, stunned, "What day is it today?"

"Friday. Upalbabu, tell Subinoy that if he makes any trouble for Preeti we shall have no option but to request police protection. Preeti is now someone else's legal wife."

"Don't say someone," I shook my head. I did not like the word 'someone'. I added with conviction, "Preeti is my wife."

"Wife on paper." Ruma said sharply.

"No, no," the ex-lover spoke up. "Upalbabu is right. Preeti is now his wife."

Preeti was still crying inconsolably, her head on the table. Waves of compassion rocked my heart. But the wall of people stood blocking my way.

I pleaded, "Please let me go to her once. She is my wife … my wife is crying."

The ex-lover said, "Let her cry. These are tears of joy. Now let's talk about the important things. You will have to show the marriage certificate to Subinoy. Face him like a hero. Remember that you are fighting for your wife's safety."

I nodded sagely and said, "I understand. But Subinoy won't do anything. He is scared of me."

And upon that, I started to laugh.

The ex-lover said, "We know that Upalbabu. We know he is scared of you because you are privy to many of his secrets. And that is the reason you have been chosen for this job."

"Chosen!" I gulped a mouthful of air and asked, "What do you mean?"

"Slip of the tongue, my dear." The ex-lover laughed a little and said, "Don't mind. Now listen carefully. You will also inform Subinoy that Preeti is not going to the States day after tomorrow. Instead, Preeti and you are leaving for your honeymoon tomorrow … to the Kulu valley."

"Kulu Valley?"

"Yes. You will mislead Subinoy. He will try to follow you; and in that case, you will leave Kolkata. It is not safe for Subinoy to be in the city till Preeti leaves. He is dangerous."

I nodded. The ex-lover fished out a bundle of notes and stuffed it into my pocket, "For your expenses, five thousand."

I said in surprise, "Money! But why? Why should you pay me to assure the safety of my wife?"

"Wife on paper," Ruma said again.

"Oh no," the ex-lover said. "Of course she is your wife but the need for money may arise anyway. Keep it as a gift."

I hesitated. Money! Lots of money! Had money really become so cheap in the world? Of late, I was being showered with money at every turn, like free falling handbills.

The ex-lover rested a hand on my back and tried to guide me towards the door. But I stood my ground like a stubborn mule.

Preeti raised her face, wiped her eyes and looked at me. Her eyes were red. Her face was dark with pent up emotion. Her lips moved. Did she say something? No sound came out but I guessed what she said. "Poor thing!"

I shrugged off the ex-lover's hand and advanced towards Preeti, and said, "Preeti dear, don't worry. I'll do everything I can for you."

I floated towards Preeti as she gazed at me with a dazed look in her eyes. I said, "Preeti, my wife!"

All of a sudden Ruma blocked my way with lightning speed. She said in a hard voice, "Upalbabu, leave Preeti alone."

My anger flared and my entire body roared to life like an abruptly started motor vehicle. "Move away!" I said.

Ruma lifted her hand in her well-known 'smashing' pose and said, "Not a step further."

Past experience made me cringe. The memories of Dalmia Park throbbed like an old unhealed wound. The ex-lover came to me and held my hand. Then he said in a consoling voice, "First get the job done. Everything else will follow. Preeti is yours but right now it is more important to save her from impending dangers."

I nodded. Then I whispered into the ex-lover's ear, "You know, I have never been married before. I am feeling very happy."

He led me down the stairs as he said, "I know. You are a very nice man. You are one of the few good men left in this world."

Fourteen

Subinoy raised his head and looked at me. The smoke from his cigarette created a haze around him. The smell of alcohol wafted in the room like incorporeal souls. The room appeared blurred.

I called out to him in a shaky voice, "Subinoy!"

"Yup, buddy," Subinoy said and hiccupped.

"I have to tell you something."

The gurgling sound of liquid being poured into a glass reached me. Then I heard the scraping of a matchstick and a flame flared for a second before dying away.

Subinoy said, "Upal, I can't get myself drunk. I have been drinking since morning. Why do you think I am not drunk yet?"

"Subinoy, what I have to say is very important."

"What is it?"

"I have married Preeti."

Subinoy sighed heavily. The tip of his cigarette glowed for an instant as he said, "Congratulations."

"I am not kidding, Subinoy. Preeti is now my wife, my legal wife. Look, here is the certificate."

Subinoy reached for the piece of paper. He looked at it well and then flung it down on the table. "Damn fool," he said.

"Who?"

Subinoy looked at me through the haze and said in a thick voice, "You know something buddy? You have been framed."

"Meaning?"

Subinoy shook his head and smiled, "It is a marriage on paper, buddy—simply a paper marriage. And you are the scapegoat."

My head spun. Yet I said with as much conviction as I could muster, "No Subinoy, Preeti loves me. She has promised to be a traditional, good wife to me. She will take me to America." Subinoy's laughter gushed forth like a waterfall. He picked up the marriage certificate, scrunched it up into a ball and threw it at me, saying. "Go and frame it for your wall."

I opened out the scrunched up paper and tried to smooth down the creases. I said, "Preeti is now my wife, Subinoy. Don't disturb us."

Subinoy spoke as he lay sprawled on the sofa, "I won't Upal. Sit down."

I took a seat.

Subinoy said in a far-away voice, "So Preeti is leaving day after?"

"No, no. We are leaving for the Kulu valley tomorrow, on our honeymoon," I parroted.

He laughed, "I can smell the truth, buddy. Don't lie."

I felt frightened. My self-confidence waned and I broke out in sweat.

Subinoy sat up and asked, "Upal, why is she resorting to these immature tricks? They are of no use. If I so wish, I can easily stop her from leaving. I can send her lover to the hospital for a good six months."

A motor car inside me started to life. Rage roared within me.

I said in a suppressed voice, "Subinoy! Careful!"

Subinoy said, "No one can stop me."

My senses took leave of me and I advanced towards him, a step at a time. I said, "I don't want to hear another word about Preeti. She is my wife."

Subinoy hiccupped and then laughed.

Without a shred of hesitation, I aimed a kick at his face and shouted, "Scoundrel!"

The booted kick caught his chin. Subinoy grunted and clamped both his hands on his chin. The second kick landed on his head. He swayed slightly and collapsed on the sofa. I leapt on him like a tiger and caught his throat in a vicelike grip with both hands. "I'll kill you, you filthy dog. I'll kill you."

I grated my teeth as Subinoy looked at me, stunned.

I summoned all my strength to tighten my hold on his throat. He had a thick muscular neck; but what of it, I had to do what I had to do. I tried to strangle him with all my might as I repeated, "Die! Die! Die!"

Subinoy did not try to stop me. He shook me off easily and sat up. I landed on the rug with a thud.

Without sparing me a glance he picked up his glass and took a swig.

"You are a fool, Upal. You could hardly guess that they sent you here to be thrashed by me."

I sat up slowly. My head was reeling. I hadn't eaten in a long while.

Subinoy fixed me with his stare and then shook his head, "But I am not going to hit you for Preeti. She is not my problem. I want to know what you have done to Khawna."

I sat on the sofa across from him. The rage ebbed away and my body felt awash with fatigue. I held my head in my hands and said, "I did not do anything, Subinoy. I only did what you asked me to do."

Subinoy filled up his glass and lit another cigarette.

"Upal."

"Hmm."

"Khawna is spoilt … thoroughly spoilt," Subinoy said and stared at me with a strange look in his eyes—of anxiety, abhorrence and awe. After a long while he said sharply, "You demon! You devil! What have you done to Khawna?"

His tone sent a shiver through me. My voice appeared to have vanished.

Subinoy unfolded his giant frame and stood up. He looked monstrous. I shrunk into myself and gazed at him, as if in the grip of a spell.

"Khawna was completely mine. She did whatever I wanted her to do and behaved the way I wished her to. She was the epitome of obedience. When she looked at me her eyes shone bright. It was beautiful. She never looked at another man in the world. But last night she turned blue in fear at the sight of me. She did not come near; neither did she meet my eyes. She averted her gaze time and again. What have you done, Upal?"

I held up my hands to shield off any blows and said, "Look Subinoy …"

Subinoy took two steps forward and said, "What?"

I opened my mouth wide and gestured for him to look inside. He did and then asked, "What is it?"

"Don't you see?"

"No! What are you trying to show me inside your mouth?"

I exhaled and said, "The reflection of the universe and of time … the way Arjun saw it in Lord Krishna's mouth. If you could see that you would realise that what was destined to happen, has happened. My role is insignificant."

Subinoy gripped the glass in his hands so hard that it shattered. His eyes shot explosive darts at me. He said, "Which universe did you introduce Khawna to? How did you spoil her?"

"What could I do, Subinoy? You made me do everything."

Subinoy shook his head, "How can Khawna get spoilt? How can she love you instead of me? How is that possible?"

Subinoy strode forward and pulled me up by my shirt. He dragged me into light and took a good look at me. Then he hissed, "What is it about you? What did Khawna see in you? Tell me, you bastard, what have you done to her?"

The collar of my shirt cut into my throat and I gasped for breath. Subinoy looked deep into my eyes and tried to read me. Again he asked, "What have you done to my Khawna? Why doesn't she love me anymore? Tell me … tell me."

He released me momentarily. I straightened up only to be knocked back by a punch from Subinoy.

The drone of crickets slowly engulfed my consciousness and darkness drew me gradually into its depths. I heard Subinoy's faint voice repeat like a nagging beggar, "Give me back my Khawna … give her back to me."

•

MY ENTIRE BODY was submerged in a pool of aches and pains. My head felt empty yet heavy. I groaned and tried to sit up. I reached out and felt a pillar, and held on to it. My eyes were unable to focus properly but through the haze I saw the stairs leading up to the first floor. I had rolled down those very stairs to my present position.

The staircase looked back at me with pity and said, "That which can be used to climb down, can also be used to climb up. But you, Upal dear, don't try to climb up these stairs again. You have lost this shelter of yours."

I nodded at the staircase. I understood.

I held on to my waist and somehow managed to reach the road, my frame bent at various angles. The vast sky and the open road.… Besides these, what did I have in the world? The world seemed a very nice place.

But my conscience was not to let this opportunity slip by. It crept up from behind and whispered in my ear, "There is still some more. A lot more in store."

I shoved my hands into my pockets and felt the crunch of notes worth thousands.

My conscience prodded, "Get a taxi, Upal. Splurge some."

My tongue had a deep cut. I spit out the clotted blood. There were bumps on my temple and one eye was swollen shut. My ribs hurt and my neck felt stiff. The limbs felt floppy.

Somehow I managed to move my injured tongue and say, "Conscience dear, everyone likes to bash me up."

A taxi stopped by me and I got into it. The driver cast me suspicious looks. I shrunk into the seat, afraid that my battered looks might make him refuse to take me on.

But, right away, I remembered that my pockets were overflowing with cash. The thought lent strength to my morale. Confidence tiptoed in. I put on a serious expression and said, "Madhu Gupta lane."

Samir and his gang, in Madhu Gupta lane, were eagerly awaiting my arrival. They were pacing the lane, full of hope, and rushed towards me as soon as the taxi pulled up.

I clutched a bundle of notes and held my hand out of the window. Swallowing the pain shooting through my tongue, I managed to say, "Leave Ketaki alone."

One of the boys leaned in through the window and said, "Do you want Ketaki? If you say, we can lift her out of there and into your taxi."

I shook my head. No. I had a wife. I would like to go to her.

Another boy now pushed his head in through the window and said, "Which son of a bitch laid a hand on you? Tell us his address. We'll take care of him."

I shook my head. I had pardoned everyone. Now I would like to go to my wife. She would gently stroke and caress my bruised body. I would fall asleep. A long, deep sleep.

I asked the taxi to turn around towards the main road. It was eight in the evening and the city was bubbling with activity. It felt like an eternal carnival. People at peace with life were gathered at the shops, at the cinemas.

I moved my wounded tongue and said, "Conscience dear, I would like to make people happier. Tonight I am going to my wife. Let everyone be happy, let them bless us."

My conscience struck a light note on his fiddle and said, "You still have a lot of money left. You wanted to spend as freely as one handed out handbills!"

Of course. I nodded.

I scooped out a bunch of notes from a bundle and flung them out the window. They were taken up by the wind like handbills. They fluttered in the air like kites. And then they slowly descended onto the brightly-lit streets and the people.

I looked out through the rear glass. The people, suddenly called to attention by the shower of money, were running with open arms to gather the notes. They hopped off hurriedly from moving trams and buses. One of them almost got run over as he ran after the money.

I flung another handful into the wind. And watched. A shopkeeper left his shop unattended. The gaudily made-up girls from the red light lane brushed aside their customers and joined the rush. A man with a fractured leg was on his way to the Medical

College hospital in a hand-pulled rickshaw. All of a sudden he leapt down from it on both legs.

I flung out another handful after the busy Bowbazar crossing.

The taxi driver stopped the car and asked, "What on earth is happening behind us?"

"Nothing. You carry on."

The driver drove on. And I continued to release the money into the wind. The city went mad as it followed me. The traffic policeman forgot his duty and joined the race. The cinema gave over and shops downed their shutters. A riot ensued. Traffic came to a standstill. A black police car chased us but I paid no heed. I scattered the notes happily again at the Chowringhee crossing.

The notes fluttered. They twirled. And then they fell to the ground.

I watched mesmerised. This was how I had always wished to see money. Should be cheap and simple to earn and be in plenty. I was so engrossed in the scene that all else slid to the background. The taxi had stopped long back. The police car was now parked beside us.

When the policemen were dragging and pulling me into their car I shouted from the bottom of my heart, "Leave me! My wife is waiting for me. I have to go to her."

An armed police officer said, "I have never seen so much black money."

•

I DON'T REMEMBER for how long I was sentenced and in jail. My mind was elsewhere when the magistrate read the sentence out.

The woollen blanket I slept on had given me an itchy skin. Hence, I was busy scratching away. After the verdict was read out, the police locked me up.

Then, one day, they released me.

It seemed quite meaningless—the locking up and then the release.

As I walked out, the outside world appeared somewhat unfamiliar. Another inmate was also released with me. We walked along together. He said, "The wretched fools."

"Who?"

"The ones who sent me to prison. Actually, I am the one who committed the murder! Not Badyinath. But well, he was the one who got a life term while I was imprisoned for six months."

He laughed out loud and said, "Let me offer prayers to goddess Kali. Then I'll take a dip in the Ganga and head home. Where are you off to?"

I stared at the dark, squat, man. Then I said, "I am confused. Can't figure out the roads. I want to go to my wife."

"Don't worry. Let's go together. Someday your wife will surely turn up."

I nodded and fell in step with him.

The man paid his respects at the temple and took a dip in the river. Then we caught a train from Kalighat station and changed trains at Sealdah. The man carried on. I followed. I have always found that once on the road, you were sure to find a companion.

We alighted at Palasi and walked over fields and uneven terrain for quite a distance. I asked, "It's all very well that you are taking me along. But will you make me toil hard?"

The man shrugged off all pretence of generosity, "What do you mean? Do you think I have fed you and paid your fares for nothing? Surely not because of your looks! I can make out that you are slightly nuts. But I can't stand a sponge. You'll be in trouble if I find you taking things too easy."

Well, this was only to be expected. I sighed. I thought, one day, when a clear picture of the road to take unfolded before my eyes, I would catch the simple road to my wife. Till then, I would wait for my head to clear.

The man burdened me with a lot of work. He had a sizeable plot of farmland which I had to irrigate by drawing water from a well. Extremely hard work it was. I also cleared weeds, swept the courtyard and fed the cattle. I didn't have a minute to spare for myself.

Many nights, sleep eluded me. I left my bed and walked out to the fields where the wind flowed free. The endless sky loomed above and the vast expanse of ground lay underneath. This self-same sky enveloped the world and this same ground stretched out under the feet of all men. They connected every man to his fellows. The thought pleased me.

Some nights, my aged conscience came to sit beside me. He said, "Upal, I would like to sing you a ballad."

"Go on."

But the moment he started to sing, a bout of coughing overtook him. And he never got around to singing the ballad for me. He gasped for breath as he said, "What a shame! Oh, by the way, the food was very nice at Ketaki's wedding. Delicious!"

"Did Ketaki cry?"

"Of course! All girls cry when they leave their maternal home."

"But she was supposed to cry for me as well."

My conscience said, "When people cry, their various sorrows mingle into one. It is hard to tell which sob is for which sorrow. But she did ask your aunt why you didn't attend. She believes that it was because of you that she was wedded well. But let that be, Upal. Let me, instead, tell you about the delicacies."

"Does Subinoy live with Khawna?"

My conscience replied excitedly, "Of course he does. You don't need to worry about them. Nowadays, they often go to the cinema and watch plays together; and whenever they have time they condemn you."

"Do you have any news of Preeti?"

"That's not too hard to gather. Upon reaching America, she filed a divorce case against you. At the time, you were in prison. Having obtained a one-sided decree she has now married her lover. Do you think they gave you five thousand rupees for nothing? But sometimes, she does say, 'Poor Upal!'"

I sighed heavily.

My conscience looked at me and said, "Do you want to hear more news? Remember Pailen, who fell off the train? Well, he didn't die … he lost a leg. Now he earns a living by making and selling cloth dolls. Haju and Kadam are still on their old track of petty thievery. Manik Saha lives in the Sunderbans, alone. He has a job on a boat and is very happy. Do you want to hear more?"

I shook my head, "No."

My conscience said, "That's what I say too. What's the use? Those are not your worries. You are your biggest worry. Let me tell you about the great food at Ketaki's wedding—the delicious pumpkin *chhokha*. Aah! The sweets—the *rasakadamba* they served!"

I slipped into a slumber as I listened to him. My conscience left in a huff.

And then, in the dark field, came the squeaks of rats, field mice and insects. They called out to one another.

I woke up too; and sat silent. Slowly, an uncanny hunger raised its head in my belly. It was an incurable hunger, quite like cancer. I realised that hunger robbed sleep all over the world—rats, humans, insects … hunger woke them all up.

The moon rose in the sky. I gazed at it. The rats, too, stared at it. I said, "I am very hungry."

My words spread in all directions with lightning speed. From all corners of the world animals and humans spoke up in unison, "We are not troubled by matters of the heart. Neither by philosophy, science or love. It is only hunger which troubles us. We are very hungry."